ALS

NUTCRACKER WITH BENEFITS

HOLIDAY RETELLINGS
BOOK 1

LIZ ALDEN

NUTCRACKER WITH BENEFITS

First Edition

Library of Congress Control Number: 2022918585

League City, Texas, United States of America

Proofread by Lisa Matsumura

Cover Design by Quamber Designs

To my grandmother, who introduced me to The Nutcracker. I'm not sure she would appreciate my medium, but whatever.

1

CLARA

It was a goddamn Christmas miracle. *I* am a goddamn Christmas miracle.

Three flights, two delays, forty-eight hours of travel time, one spilled coffee, a sprint across CDG airport, and I made it to New York City.

The doorman sends me up in the elevator to Uncle D's penthouse apartment. What is normally a brightly lit space is nearly pitch black—it's four am on Christmas morning, and Uncle D's floor-to-ceiling windows are opaque, blocking the ever-present lights of the big city. The Christmas tree isn't even lit up, although I can see the dark shape of it sulking in the corner.

I glide in, the wheels of my suitcase smoothly following behind me. Dad and Uncle D are surely asleep, and I don't want to wake them. Uncle D is fastidious about his sleep, claiming that eight hours a night is going to help him work his magic. What magic that is, since he's practically retired now, I don't know.

But there is one person sleeping here that I don't mind waking. I leave my luggage by the door, gently setting down my backpack next to it and slipping my shoes off. I walk in the opposite direction from Dad and Uncle D's room toward the west wing of the penthouse. This side is more familiar to me; one of these bedrooms will be mine for a few days, my home in New York while I celebrate the holidays with my family. But the other bedroom is even more familiar—Nash's room.

I gently turn the knob on the door, the soft glow from the flashlight on my phone illuminating a dark shape on the bed. I leave it on just long enough to make out the edge, Nash's dark head of hair peeking out from under the white comforter. Nash's bedding must be new because the last time I was here, it was navy.

The door closes with a soft click. I tiptoe over the mattress, resting a knee on the bed, and then carefully crawling up.

"Hey, baby," I say gently. The body shifts next to me. Nash has always been a light sleeper, even with the blackout windows and high-end bed that he keeps now.

I lean down closer. "I finally made it. Want to welcome Christmas in the naughty way?"

Nash raises up, and I can barely see anything, but I bet he's got the adorable, grumpy, and sleepy face that he gets when he's been woken up. I know it pretty well after nine years of booty calls, and I know that Nash, when he fully wakes up, will be thrilled to see me, and even more thrilled with the wake-up call.

My voice turns playful, and I give the sheets a little tug. "Come on, Nash, wakey, wakey. We have a few hours before my dads wake up."

The grip on the sheets turns firm, and a voice I definitely did not expect answers me.

"Clara?" the man in bed says to me.

"Dad?"

2

NASH

I whistle "Dance of the Sugar Plum Fairies" as Frank opens the door to the building for me. I'm about to spend Christmas with some of my favorite people in the world; my mentor and boss, Uncle D, his husband Craig, and their daughter Clara. Hell, I'm even happy to see Clara's brother Fritz and his family, even though Fritz and I don't get along.

"Merry Christmas, Frank," I say.

He tips his cap at me, his old-school white gloves firmly gripping the shiny bill. "Merry Christmas, Nash. Clara got in early and I expect Fritz and company are minutes behind you."

"I suspect so, too," I say, taking an envelope out of my pocket. I'm sure Uncle D tips the building staff well during the holidays, but I've known Frank for years, known his wife and kids, too. It would be weird not to give him a bonus, even if I don't live here anymore. "Tell Alison and the kids Merry Christmas," I say.

"Thank you, sir," he says, eyebrows shooting up in surprise.

The elevator is quick to come, and I press the button for Uncle D's penthouse as the doors close.

I inspect my reflection in the stainless steel as the elevator shoots up. Clara and I used to have fun competing for the most outlandish pajamas to wear on Christmas day, and this year I've gone a little over the top. I found a set that illustrates *Grandma Got Run Over by a Reindeer*, with an elderly woman holding a mug of beer and Santa cracking his whip over the team of reindeer. The background is bright blue, making the pajamas garish and hard to miss.

Now that Fritz's kids are old enough to pick out their own pajamas, the tradition has grown to include the whole family. Though I don't think Fritz's wife, Whitney, will be pleased with me for having to explain the song to her kids.

I've been celebrating Christmas with my boss's family for nine years. It's hard to think of Rolf, the man I, and his family, affectionately call Uncle D, as my boss, especially now that he's been easing into retirement. But he is still my boss.

And Clara, his stepdaughter, is the woman I've loved for the past few years. It's been hard, though: in college, Clara started a food and travel blog, and after graduation, armed with a journalism degree, Clara went full time, traveling the world and leaving us—especially me—behind.

I'm not bitter about it. Clara's fulfilling a dream her mother never got to pursue. But god, I miss her every day, and I'm excited to see her today. Excited and nervous because I have plans for us to do something completely different.

The elevator opens right into the penthouse, and I step in, taking my boots off at the rack in the foyer. "Hello?" I call. The space is quiet, the ding of the elevator having announced my arrival.

There's a moment of silence, one that feels heavy for a reason I can't fathom, and then Uncle D calls back, "In the kitchen."

I shed my coat and sweater before wandering in, but the tension in the room is thick and makes me pause. Clara, still in her athleisure wear from the flight, is perched on a barstool, looking like she would rather be anywhere else, while Uncle D and her father stand across the kitchen island. Both of them are white men in their fifties, and while Craig has a full head of dark hair with gray sprinkled into his beard and sideburns, Rolf keeps his balding head cropped close. A frown and lines of concern at the corner of his eyes mar Craig's features. Uncle D is in a familiar stance, supportive and clearly on his husband's side, but not wanting to interfere with parenting.

"What's going on?" I ask.

They all have coffee mugs in front of them, partially full but cold and ignored.

"You're sleeping with my daughter?" Craig volleys back.

Well, I thought I was nervous before.

I glance at Clara, and though I'm guessing she's been traveling for a very long time and hasn't showered or slept in a while, she's beautiful. Her sandy-blonde hair is up in a ponytail, her face bare, and she's nervously chewing on her lip.

As a programmer, my brain is used to seeing options and playing the *what-if* game. This is a variable I hadn't seen coming. Will this help my plan or hurt it? I don't have time to think about it, but the question in front of me only has one right answer.

I raise an eyebrow, checking with Clara before I open my mouth. *Truth?*

She gives me a subtle nod, and I stand next to her, an arm going around her shoulder and our bodies touching. She leans into me slightly, and the thrill of this somewhat-public acknowledgment settles me.

"Yes, sir."

"The last time you called me 'sir' was when you first moved in with us. Were you sleeping together then?"

"No, sir."

Craig looks like he wants to ask questions—a lot of questions—but I hope he doesn't ask what this is between us. I haven't lied to Uncle D and Craig since I was nineteen when Uncle D discovered that I hadn't told them about my parents kicking me out. I promised I would never lie to him again, and I haven't. I held up my end of the bargain, and he held up his, becoming my safe space, my shelter when I didn't have anywhere else to go.

If he asks what this is between us, what my intentions are with his daughter, I'll have to tell him one of two truths.

I could tell him that I've been fucking Clara behind his back, casually, for nearly a decade.

Or I could confess that I'm in love with Clara when she isn't ready to hear it.

Uncle D places a hand on Craig's shoulder and squeezes. His smile is supportive, and while he doesn't say that he knew . . . I bet he knew.

"Okay," Craig says on a deep breath out. "Okay. I just wish you had told us about this instead of hiding your relationship. It feels like you don't trust us. And to find out this way is just jarring."

"Dad—" Clara starts but is interrupted by the dinging of the elevator arriving. Fritz and his family are here, abbreviating our conversation and swinging us back into Christmas mode.

When the elevator doors open in the small foyer, it's a flurry of kids. Normally, they're already excited to see their grandparents but add in Christmas, and it's a whole different kind of mayhem, the kind that only four-year-old kids can bring.

We brace ourselves as the twins come screaming down the hall toward the pile of presents under the tree. They're in their PJs, but we've always done presents here, so they've had to wait so long to open gifts.

"This one! Me first!" Molly shouts, and Fritz, Clara's younger brother, drops a diaper bag on the floor.

"No presents yet," Whitney says. "Say hello to Grandpa and Pop-Pop first. And Auntie Clara, you remember her?"

Uncle D, or Pop-Pop as the kids call him, squats down to give Molly and Ricky hugs.

Craig, aka Grandpa, follows, and they take turns exclaiming over the twins' wacky Christmas pajamas.

"What is that?" Craig points at the brown lump wearing a Santa hat on Ricky's pajama bottoms.

"Poop!" Ricky shouts, as pleased as a four-year-old can be.

"Mine is a T-rex!" Molly's not to be outdone.

"Whitney!" Clara says and hugs her sister-in-law awkwardly while Whitney has Benny, the five-month-old, strapped to her chest.

Clara's hug with Fritz is less comfortable. I suspect it has to do with me: when I moved in with Craig and Uncle D, Fritz was still in high school. He thought I'd be his sidekick and we'd get in trouble together, but I was more interested in the work Uncle D was offering me, and Fritz's favorite taunts quickly became calling me a suck-up and brown nose.

While he works for Heartly, he's stagnated the past few years, neither willing to put in the work or strike out on his own. He's not as close to us, and most holidays are spent with Whitney's family—except Christmas, because Whitney's family is Jewish.

And because this is the one reliable time of year Clara is in town.

We're also not that close because . . . Fritz is a dick.

"Ricky, you remember your Auntie Clara, right?" Whitney asks.

Last time Clara was visiting, Ricky was going through a shy phase, and while he'd seen Clara just two months prior, little kids' memories don't have that kind of longevity at that age. He'd barely interacted with her, and I had seen in the set of Clara's mouth and the dull of her blue eyes that it bothered her.

"We look at her pictures online?" Whitney presses.

Molly stands in front of Clara and gives her a critical look. Her eyes widen. "MOM! Clara's not wearing pajamas! You said she would be wearing pajamas!"

"For fuck's sake," Fritz mutters under his breath, loud enough to be heard by all of us, and Whitney immediately reprimands him for it. He rolls his eyes. "I knew this was a bad idea."

"Sweetie, we talked about this." Whitney bends down over Molly, who's in full meltdown mode, screaming. "It's a family tradition, and that's why you had to wear the pajamas."

Molly's screeching is at epic levels, and Clara starts backing toward the hallway.

"I just came in from the airport. I haven't even put my stuff in my room." She grabs the handle of her rolling bag. "Don't worry, Molly, I'm going to go put my pajamas on right now." She disappears down the west wing hallway.

Craig distracts the kids by showing them his new pajamas —a Where's Waldo holiday theme. This definitely works, and the kids spend a few minutes scanning Craig's legs for Waldo. Thankfully the illustration stops at the thighs, so there's no looking for Waldo in dangerous territory.

"Okay!" Clara's voice calls out from the hallway moments before she appears. "I'm in my pajamas now. Christmas has officially started. Who's ready to open presents?" The kids don't even notice Clara's pajamas. The bottoms are printed like fishnet stockings, and the fitted white shirt says *fra-gee-lay* across her chest above a lampshade. It's even got a fringed hem.

Like they've been given pogo sticks, Molly and Ricky bounce up and down, their earlier shyness and meltdown vanished.

"Nice *A Christmas Story* pajamas," I say as Clara settles next to me. Her blonde hair is up in a tight ponytail that swishes when she moves her head and is just long enough to brush my shoulder. She's got more freckles since the last time I saw her; her skin is a little tanner. There's a dimple on her left cheek that I've always loved kissing.

"Thanks. Ordered them a month ago, and Dad's been holding onto them for me."

Our attention turns to the kids. The Christmas lights have been plugged in, lighting the tree up with a soft, white glow. Craig has lit the gas fireplace and a few candles, so the smell of fir mingles with the fresh round of coffees that have been poured for the adults.

"Stockings first," Whitney cries, and the kids' eyes scan the room—looking first to the glass fireplace and then around the couch—until they locate the stockings. Too full to be held up by any stocking holder, the knitted monstrosities lean against the glass wall behind the Christmas tree.

Three of them are old and stretched, hand knit with names at the top: Clara, Fritz, and Dad. They're family treasures made by Clara's mom for her children's first Christmases. In an album, somewhere, there are family photos of both Clara and Fritz as infants, each bundled into their respective stockings.

Yes, they are that big.

The remaining ones—Rolf, Nash, Whitney, Ricky, Molly, and Benny—gradually grow newer. It's Benny's first Christmas, and his stocking, bought by Craig and Uncle D, was made from a knitting shop in The Village.

"Who's going to help Santa by handing out stockings?" Whitney asks as she unstraps Benny from her chest. It takes some time, but eventually, everyone ends up with the right stocking.

"On the count of three," Craig says. He and Uncle D are seated next to each other on the couch, stockings in their lap. Molly and Ricky are on the edge of their seats, fingers twitching to grab and rip and consume.

"One, two, three!" the three of them shout together, and we all tear into our presents.

I know what's in my stocking, or most of it anyway: chocolate oranges, gold-wrapped chocolate coins, pomegranates, and toys and miniatures for the hottest video games. The food I'll likely share with Clara, but the toys I'll end up donating. Of course, Craig and Uncle D know this, but they keep it up every year.

Ricky lets out a shriek when he finds one of the toys I picked out for him wrapped up in paper; a wind-up toy mouse. He's at the age where pranks are *hilarious*. I just hope Whitney thinks it's funny; the mouse is disturbingly realistic.

"Well, well, well. Look what I have here," Clara says next to me. Her gifts are usually food, too, since she travels light. But when I look over, she's pulling out a glossy cylinder from her stocking.

The magazine unfurls, and I groan. "Oh no."

"Oh, yes. I heard all about this, and now I get an advanced copy?"

I shoot a mock glare at Uncle D, and he shrugs. The gift is from him.

"What is it?" Fritz asks. Clara holds it up for the room to see—it's Forbes magazine's upcoming edition. On the cover is my face, close-cropped and solemn.

Fritz rolls his eyes and gets back to helping Ricky with the mouse. Despite the tension between me and Fritz, I have to admit he's a great family man. He's super patient in helping his son, the shyest kid I have ever known, get his toys set up.

"'Social Media's Nutcracker'," Clara reads from the story title. She leans back, the rest of her stocking falling to the floor, forgotten.

"Have you read this?" she asks me.

"A digital version. I haven't seen it in print yet."

"You can have my copy when I leave." My heart drops at

the mention of her leaving, a pain I've grown used to ignoring. Clara clears her throat. "Now, let's see here . . ."

I lean back against Clara, taking the opportunity to press against her side and read over her shoulder.

"'Social media has swept its toxic reputation away, thanks to the team behind the social media company Heartly, spearheaded by Nash Darwish.' They went very dramatic on this spread." She lifts the left side toward me, where I can see my own eyes staring back at me again; this time it's in the glow of a screen, and the rest of my face is hidden behind a laptop.

Clara reads the article, mostly to herself, providing commentary as she goes. ". . . algorithms discouraging toxic activity, all a part of the coding created by Darwish."

All right, I hate the idea of the article in general, but these words, especially as read by Clara, make my chest swell.

She knows the story, of course—that in Heartly's office, under the direction of Rolf, we became obsessed with how to turn social media from a place where negativity was spread to a place where good things happened—without losing audience. Rolf treated it like a puzzle, telling us every step we took was one step closer to cracking the code. He made everything at Heartly a game, and every little piece of the puzzle we figured out was a nut to crack.

"I like this bit about you reframing the hiring process for including more diverse applicants and the work visa program," she says.

"It was good work," Uncle D agrees.

A minute later, Clara snorts. "That's very diplomatic of you." She points to a line, and I read it. *"My birth family and I don't see eye to eye on a lot of topics," Nash says.*

I shrug. "They wanted to talk more about my parents, but fortunately, our PR team vetoed a lot of those questions."

"Smart," Clara says, nodding.

The PR people also carefully helped me craft answers that wouldn't invite questions. It was hard to talk about why the work visa program and computer science camps for kids were so important without bringing up my parents, who are ultra-conservative and restricted my education growing up.

Clara always hated my dad, which was understandable. "I would have used some choice words of my own, but they probably couldn't print those," she says.

The final straw for me with my parents had been when Clara and I were sixteen and my dad called her feltene—loose. She didn't know about that, of course, but the way they treated my sister was enough to have Clara's hackles up. My sister is the only reason I still have any form of relationship with them—I hope that she sees the light someday. But so far, she's resistant and spewing as much misogynistic crap as they do.

"Oh my god, we even get a mention! 'Drosselmeyer has been a father figure to Darwish since he discovered the fifteen-year-old reading books on computer science while his father cleaned the office building.'"

While my dad did his janitorial duties for Heartly, the social media company Rolf founded, he would tell me to sit in an empty office and pray. I wasn't a troublemaker, but it didn't take long for me to find programming textbooks in offices and crack them open. Rolf found me one night when he was working late and has nurtured my education ever since, despite my dad's disapproval.

It wasn't long after Rolf and I started late-night tutorials that I met Clara. We didn't know what to make of each other at first—me, a gangly Arabic kid who was often angry at God and my parents, and Clara, a sweet-natured girl with an adoring family.

Clara keeps reading; "'Drosselmeyer and his husband, Craig Cohen, are the found family Darwish needed to encourage his intellectual pursuits. Darwish considers Cohen's kids, Clara and Fritz, his siblings.'"

She sputters on the last sentence, and Craig chokes on his

coffee, too. I had tried to argue against that phrasing because I definitely *do not* see Clara as my sister, but after a few back-and-forth emails about it, it got to be a *he doth protest too much* situation, and I let it go.

The line is awkward by itself, but now, in the context of Rolf and Craig knowing about us, it's downright mortifying.

But the verbiage is forgotten when Clara flips the page. "Awe, look at the photo they included."

She turns the magazine around to show the room. It's a picture of Uncle D, Craig, me, and Clara at a gala event last year.

"Which event was this?" Whitney asks, squinting at the page.

Clara flips it back around. "It just says 'an event in Los Angeles.'" She turns to me. "Do you remember?"

I look down at the photo. Clara's wearing a bright blue dress, the slit in the skirt showing off her legs and glittering heels. She's laughing—we both are—and sandwiched between us are Craig and Uncle D, gazing at each other adoringly.

"That was the gala for the refugee center," I say. "Whitney, you weren't there because you were on bed rest with Benny."

What I don't say is that the most memorable part of the night wasn't the event itself, but later. Clara didn't attend events like that one often, because she was usually in some inconvenient part of the world. But this time she'd been in Guam, a non-stop flight away from LA, and I'd offered to pay for the ticket so she could come for the weekend. Most places she travels to are three flights and long layovers, and she can't get home as easily. The event being on the West Coast certainly helped this time.

After Craig and Uncle D had decided they'd spent enough time—and money—at the gala, they'd departed, and Clara and I waited about five minutes before making our own exit.

And then my memories are the NSFW variety—taking

advantage of that slit in her dress by making her come in the elevator; hoisting Clara up against the window in my suite, the cold glass causing goosebumps to break out across her skin; my breath fogging the view as I thrust into her, a bokeh effect turning the cityscape even more magical.

Craig glances up and it's clear as day on his face that he's wondering about my relationship with Clara in this picture. My cheeks heat. Not only am I thinking inappropriate thoughts, but he's probably wondering what I'm thinking about.

Clara shoots her brother and Whitney an apologetic look. That was a tough time for them; with Whitney on bedrest and the twins in their terrible twos, the rest of us had tried to figure out a way for one of us to stay to help, but both Fritz and Whitney insisted they were fine.

"God, I loved that dress," she says, gazing at the photo. I loved it, too. "Kara always did such a great job picking out stuff for me. How is she?"

Kara is the personal stylist I've been using for years, ever since I started to take on a more forward-facing role at the company and I could afford it. Well, it took a gentle nudge from Uncle D to get me to cave—I hadn't wanted to spend the money, but the press was starting to pay more attention to me, and unflattering photos were appearing in magazines, sometimes labeled as what *not* to wear.

They were very unforgiving about my dal-stained University of Washington sweatshirt, the one that Clara gave me for Christmas her freshman year. They called my look "Middle Eastern Frat Boy."

"Kara is doing great, but you can ask her yourself tomorrow."

Clara perks up next to me. "We're going to see Kara? You're sharing me with someone else?"

Oops. I'd let a hint slip.

"Wow." She elongates the word, drawing it out.

"Are you two seriously still doing this?" Fritz teases.

"Yes, we are," Clara says haughtily. "It's fun. And tradition."

We started this when I moved with Craig and Uncle D to New York City. Heartly's office was moving from Dover to Manhattan, which was the catalyst for my fall out with my parents. They'd denied me an education, I'd lost Clara when she went off to school, and then I was losing the next best things in my life—Rolf and Heartly, where I was working part-time.

That first Christmas living with them, Clara came home, and I hadn't seen her in sixteen months. We knew that her time would be precious when she was visiting, but neither of us wanted to sacrifice spending time with each other. So we agreed that, whenever we could, we'd spend an entire day together.

Sometimes it didn't work out—Clara might be in town for less than thirty-six hours, or I might have a big meeting or conference or some such thing that couldn't be ignored.

But the day together also gave us an excuse to be away from the rest of the family—and no one blinked an eye when Clara slept over at my apartment.

It was those days together, away from her family and the office, that led to our first time sleeping together.

"What are we doing tomorrow?" Clara asks, eyes filled with curiosity and dragging me away from an inappropriate trip down memory lane. Over the past nine years, we've done everything from strip monopoly in my place on a rainy day to visiting the Sex Museum on Fifth Avenue and doing some at-home experiments, from babysitting for Fritz and Whitney together to picnicking in Central Park.

It's been nine years, but I'm lucky if I get two days a year with her.

This time, though, I have a mission: a mission to show

Clara that New York can be so much more than a quick stopover for her. That New York could be everything to her.

"You'll have to wait to find out," I say.

Clara returns to reading the article. For a few minutes, she reads in silence while the rest of us chat until Clara forcefully puts the magazine down, a finger between the pages holding her place. Her eyes dance, and I prepare myself for the incoming tease.

"Where did they get these numbers from?" She gestures with the magazine.

"What numbers?"

She picks it back up and reads it aloud. "'The company owes so much of its success to Nash that he is the third highest-paid employee, paid even more than Drosselmeyer. Darwish is on track to become a billionaire by the age of thirty.' A billionaire!" Clara crows.

"Really?" Fritz asks from the corner.

"It's not—"

"Look at you, you fancy billionaire." Clara interrupts my protests. "If only they could see you now with your drunk granny pajamas."

"I'm not a billionaire," I say firmly.

"Fine. An almost-billionaire. Ooooo."

I roll my eyes. My cheeks are burning.

Clara keeps reading. She must be almost to the end by now, and my heart rate picks up, wondering what she'll think when she reads the last few lines.

I watch her read, her brow growing more furrowed. She darts a glance up at me, frowning.

Our gazes hold for a moment, and then Clara flashes me a smile—is it wistful? Hopeful? I can't tell.

She snaps the magazine closed. "Okay, should we get lunch ready?"

Disappointment sinks into my stomach, but what did I

expect? We're surrounded by her family, and it's Christmas. Of course, she doesn't want to talk about the implications.

"That sounds great," Whitney says. "Fritz, you have the kids?"

"Yup," he says, barely looking up from playing with Ricky.

Whitney gazes adoringly at her husband and climbs to her feet. Uncle D and Craig rise, too. Craig tugs Uncle D's arm and whispers something to him before heading away from the kitchen, out toward the balcony. Uncle D follows Clara and Whitney, and I planned to join them, but . . .

Craig stands outside, a slump to his shoulders. He should be in the kitchen with us, with his family, but instead, he's out there alone?

Something's not right. Is Craig upset about me and Clara?

I consider asking Uncle D, but instead, I tell myself to grow a pair and ask Craig myself. While I'm not as close to Craig as I am to Uncle D, I trust that if he doesn't want to talk to me, he'll tell me.

Craig glances back when I open the door. He's got a loose cardigan on, not much to protect against the cold, so I can't imagine he'll be out here for long.

"Hey," he says.

I shove my hands into the pockets of my pajama bottoms, glad I have my thick socks on.

"Are you okay?"

He shakes his head slightly. "I guess this thing with you and Clara has messed with my head."

"I'm sorry," I say, trying to keep it simple when it's anything but.

Craig eyes me. "That thing you said in the article. You were talking about Clara, weren't you?"

"Yes."

Craig frowns. "When I read the article, I just assumed that it was PR drivel. But with context now . . ."

I'm not sure what to say to that, so I don't say anything.

"It's—" he starts and shakes his head as if to clear it, beginning again. "I always thought—hoped, maybe—that someday Clara would see the wonderful man you are and something would happen between you. Nash, you have to know that Rolf and I deeply respect you and love you. I thought you might give Clara another reason to stay longer, visit more. I'm very proud of her and of the business she's built on her own, but I miss her so goddamn much sometimes." He runs a hand through his hair and stares out toward the skyline.

"With or without me, no matter where Clara is, she loves you so much," I tell him.

Craig gives me a tremulous smile. "I love her so much, too." His gaze lands on something behind me, inside his home; I can picture the idyllic family scene, full of warmth and laughter, Fritz playing with the kids, and on the other side of the penthouse, Whitney, Clara, and Uncle D working in harmony in the kitchen.

"You know," I say, "you've done a very good job of not meddling. Couldn't you have helped me out a little? Not too much meddling, just the right amount?"

Craig smiles like I hoped he would, but then he asks me a question I'm not ready to answer. "Do you love her?"

I give Craig a *look*. I haven't told Clara I love her. I'm not going to tell him first.

"Sorry." He shrugs sheepishly. "Had to ask. You know Clara's never really talked about marriage or kids . . ."

I return his shrug. "Neither have I. I'd like to get married someday." I smile. "To the right person."

"Someday," he says, hopeful.

"Someday," I echo.

3

CLARA

I HAVEN'T HAD A MOMENT TO PULL NASH ASIDE, BUT I CAN probably get him alone with the whole family divided up and occupied with their tasks.

Awkwardness has hung overhead all morning. I caught Dad glancing between Nash and me at least four times like he's trying to solve a puzzle or read a deeper meaning into everything we say.

I've tried to keep things normal, but it feels like everything has a deeper meaning now. At least Whitney and my brother seem oblivious, and the kids are a great distraction.

Uncle D and Dad had Christmas Eve dinner catered last night—which I missed, fuck you very much, Pan-Euro Airways, for the flight delay—and lunch today is leftovers. My job is to get the giant rolls ready, which will be used for sandwiches along with the leftover prime rib and turkey.

With the rolls in the oven, I have fifteen minutes until they are done. Nash and Dad are still out on the balcony, so I lean onto the counter and watch, just trying to stay out of the way. Uncle D and Whitney do a dance so smooth it looks practiced, pulling dishes out of the fridge, slicing meats, pulling veggies in and out of the microwave.

Compared to them, I feel clumsy, uncoordinated. I haven't spent the hours together in this kitchen that they have, learning their dance.

That's one of the many sacrifices for my job.

Outside the huge glass windows, I can see Dad's face—the frown and the thousand-yard stare. I wonder if Dad can see us inside or if he's frowning at his own reflection. Whichever it is, he's listening intently while Nash talks.

All I can see is Nash's back, his body language from behind.

I should be worried about the conversation they are having, but instead, I'm distracted by the view. Damn, even those ridiculous pajama pants make his butt look good. I tilt my head in appreciation.

Dad finally looks over at Nash, and whatever Nash has said he earned him a shoulder clap from my dad. They both nod, some kind of agreement reached, and Nash turns around, opening the sliding glass.

I spin around. "I'm going to use the bathroom," I say, jerking a thumb over my shoulder.

"Okay," Whitney throws casually back without removing her eyes from the buttons on the microwave, but Uncle D glances up and then over my shoulder, where Nash is coming inside.

"Don't take too long," he says, a glint of teasing in his eyes. His laissez-faire attitude about this makes me think Uncle D knew—or at least suspected—something was up with Nash and me.

I roll my eyes. Great, now that my parents know, they're going to be insufferable.

When Nash's gaze meets mine, I jerk my head toward the hallway and my room. He gives me a nod, and I walk down the hall to my room.

As I wait perched on the edge of my bed, I think back to other times we've had to do the hide-and-sneak-around thing. It was always a secret because we didn't want to make a big deal out of it.

Nash and I kept our own expectations low. I always knew that I was going to strike out on my own, do things that would take me beyond New York City, and Nash was loyal to Uncle D. I knew he'd stay here.

The door soundlessly opens, and Nash comes into the room, shutting it behind him. He glances down at me, his eye positively twinkling in amusement.

"You fucker," I hiss, sitting up straight. "Why didn't you tell me you weren't sleeping here last night?"

Nash sobers for a moment, settling in to sit next to me. "I am sorry about that. It just slipped my mind. I definitely didn't expect you to creep into bed with me."

I whack him on the arm with the back of my hand, feeling my cheeks heating. "I thought it would be sexy."

Nash glances over at my closed door and then leans in. "It definitely would have been sexy."

When he pulls back, our eyes catch for a moment. All the fire I felt this morning, excitement at the possibility of seeing Nash that banked when I stumbled into Dad instead, starts to catch again.

But a small voice in the back of my head reminds me that Nash didn't tell me he was sleeping at his place. It would have taken mere seconds to message me about it. And then there's the article . . . .

Molly screeches loud enough to be heard all the way back here, and Nash and I both jump.

When I look back at him, he's watching me, eyes full of warmth. *Don't read too much into it, Clara,* I tell myself sternly. *He's your best friend. Who you bang. Best friend with bangifits.*

I lean toward him. "When did Dad and Uncle D start sleeping separately anyway?"

"What? Oh." Nash blinks and focuses on our conversation. "Uncle D started using a CPAP at night to combat his sleep apnea. The machine keeps your dad awake, so they sleep in separate rooms."

"Oh." I nibble my lip. "Are they doing okay?"

When Nash looks down at me quizzically, he registers the concern on my face and softens. He gently bumps his shoulder with mine. "Of course they're okay. It's Uncle D and Craig. Uncle D has been scaling back his time in the office, and Craig is loving that."

Relief courses through me. "Good. Dad deserves that."

Nash and I both settle our palms on the bed behind us, leaning back.

"I feel like such a shit for not telling you I was sleeping at my place," he confesses.

"It's okay. They kept your room as a shrine a lot longer than they did mine. It had to end eventually," I tease. Nash lived with my parents while I was at college after his family kicked him out. It was just a few years ago that Nash finally got his own place, but since there were enough rooms for the two of us, he always slept over for Christmas.

Nash sighs, letting his head fall back on his neck. "It's been crazy at work. It's always hard when the holidays fall together, and this year with Hanukkah ending yesterday, it was a tight fit. The guy I've been working with on implementing some new coding is Jewish, and I've been trying hard not to pull him in, but . . . " He trails off and shrugs his shoulders. "Bugs."

That one word does explain a lot. Growing up around Uncle D and later, Nash, I know there are always bugs in the code, kinks to work out.

"Will you still be able to take tomorrow off?"

"Of course. Peter is back on the job and handling things, even today."

Silence falls over us, and I work very hard not to bring up the last few paragraphs of that stupid article. I should just ask him about it, but I'm afraid the answer will be one I don't want to hear.

Combined with the fact that Nash and I hadn't talked a whole lot lately—the miscommunication about his sleeping plans being a big one—makes me think that Nash is off limits to me. And frankly, it's about time. I knew someone would snatch him up.

"All right, well, we better get back to the family. I think the rolls are almost done, and I don't want to get in trouble if they burn." I tug on the sleeve of Nash's shirt and heave myself off the bed.

The buns don't burn, so we have sandwiches at the big dining room table, my parents ignoring the wild mess that my niblings make. It makes me wonder how often Molly and Ricky are here—often enough that they have their own place setting, apparently. I miss knowing these little things, the everyday facts about my family's lives.

Our Christmas Day tradition, once presents have been opened and our big lunch has been eaten, is to sit on the couch and watch Christmas movies all day, talking, drinking tea or cider, and grazing on leftovers when we get hungry. Not surprisingly, our family is all about the food.

I usually spend at least half the time stealing glances at Nash, and most of those are catching him looking at me, too, which always shoots a thrill through me. But this year, Nash is on the other side of the couch with Dad and Uncle D between us. Now that they know that we're more than friends, I am very conscious of trying *not* to look at Nash.

I fail. A lot.

But instead of secret glances, this year, I'm full of guilt. That last paragraph of the article plays on repeat in my head.

Darwish, who was named one of the city's most eligible bache-lors last year, says there is someone special in his life, although he declined to share details. He's been romantically linked with several women over the years, most recently Dancing with the Stars alumna Nikita Howley. But he's tight-lipped about the specifics of their relationship. "It's between me and her," he said.

Coming home has always been a mixed bag of emotions for me. I'm excited to see my family, happy to force myself to take time off from work, and always, *always* nervous-excited to see Nash.

I live in the constant fear that someday, a few days before I fly home to visit again, he'll say that, oh, he's seeing someone, so this time we won't be hooking up.

Because how is he still single?

Despite the attire du jour being Christmas pajamas—and though Nash's Christmas pajamas, with their drunken grandmas and speeding sleighs, are particularly hideous—Nash still looks every bit the confident man I've watched him grow into. He's sitting on the couch, an arm lying along the back, hand nearly touching Dad. One sock-clad foot is propped up on his knee, and he looks relaxed. But he could just as easily be wearing his suit, posing for one of the magazines. His brown skin, Roman nose, and thick eyebrows combine into a handsome face, despite the floppy hairstyle he's wearing today and the overly long growth on his face that underscores how much work he's been putting in lately.

Nash catches me staring and winks. He would have told me if he was seeing someone, right? Maybe there was someone and they broke up.

I spend the entirety of the first movie going back and forth in my mind, trying to convince myself to ask the question but also not wanting to know the answer. Schrödinger's cat: Nash is both all mine and not.

At the end of *A Charlie Brown Christmas*, the twins and Whitney have a whispered conversation, and before anyone can suggest the next movie, Whitney stands and comes to sit beside me, kids trailing along.

"Auntie Clara, Molly and Ricky have some questions for

you," she says as she props an elbow up on the back of the couch. "Who wants to go first?"

"Me!" Molly says. No surprise, she often leads the charge.

"Okay," I say, clapping my hands together and leaning my elbows on my knees. "What's your question?"

"Um. Mom says that you ate a spider." Molly gazes up at me, her eyes big and round, blue just like her mother's.

"I did. I ate a spider, and I also ate a cockroach and a cricket and a few other things." I leave my list of unusual delicacies short because I do not want to explain things like bull testicles and eyeballs to four-year-olds.

"Yeah, but why?" she asks, and her little body sways back and forth while she waits for my answer.

"You know how there's a lot of different types of food you can eat? Like your dad likes Italian food and your mom likes sushi?"

Molly nods.

"I was in a country where they eat those things just like you eat potato chips."

"But why?"

Ah, so Molly is in the *why* phase now. Thankfully I'm saved by Ricky.

"Harry eats crickets."

I blink at Ricky. "Who's Harry?"

"Harry's the snake that lives in our room at school."

"Ah. Well, if Auntie Clara eats crickets and Harry eats crickets, then maybe crickets are delicious." I spread my hands and make an exaggerated *maybe* face.

"But," Whitney hastens to add, "we don't eat Harry's crickets, okay?"

"Right, right. So Harry probably eats his crickets alive?" I ask the kids.

They both nod.

"Well, Auntie Clara says you should only eat crickets

when they've been cooked properly by an adult, okay? No stealing Harry's snacks."

"Gee, thanks," Whitney adds dryly. "Someday, they're going to ask me to cook crickets for them."

"Sorry," I say, not at all sorry. I prop my elbow on my knee and my chin on my hand.

She smirks at me. "Just wait for the next question. We've been having some conversations about sexuality, so brace yourself." She turns back to her children. "Ricky, what is your question for Auntie Clara?"

Ricky grips my knee, getting up close to me. "Mom and Dad say that Grandpa is a bicycle."

I quickly uncurl my hand to try to hide my smile. I don't want Ricky to think I'm laughing at him, but holy shit that's hysterical. The rest of the room struggles to hold their laughter, too. Fritz, in the corner, trying to build one of Molly's Christmas gifts, outright chortles, and the couch shakes underneath me, Uncle D trying to hold back his laughter.

Whitney, with the patience of a saint, gently corrects Ricky. "He's bisexual, sweetie."

"Bicycle," Ricky repeats.

I glance over at Nash, whose eyes are twinkling with mirth.

"Yes," I say, turning my attention back to my very serious nephew. "Grandpa is bisexual."

"And him and Pop-Pop are married." Ricky's scratches at his chin, and then he pinches his lip.

"Yes," I say, wondering where this is going.

"Why do you call him Uncle D?" he asks.

"We recently also learned about stepdads," Whitney explains.

"Ah, okay. Well, my dad and Uncle D have been best friends for a very long time. And sometimes, when you're best friends with someone, your kids might call them aunt or uncle to make them part of the family."

Ricky and Molly both nod, big exaggerated movements like they don't know how heavy their heads are.

"So when I was your age, I started calling him my uncle, but I had a hard time saying Uncle Drosselmeyer. Can you say Drosselmeyer?"

"Drothlmay!" Molly shouts. Ricky's finger comes out of his mouth and wriggles up to his nose.

"Ricky, we don't pick our noses while we talk to people," Whitney reminds him.

"Close," I tell Molly. "It's kind of a hard name, right? So he told me I should call him Uncle D, which is a *lot* easier to say. Now, do you want to know a little secret?"

I lean in, and the kids lean in too because they are at the age where secrets are *super exciting*, but they can't keep one to save their lives, as I discovered last time I was in town and told them the extra slice of cake was "our little secret." Molly, god bless her, tried her best not to tell her parents but didn't have the foresight to check her hair for bright blue frosting.

"When my mom passed away, Uncle D was around even more, and eventually, he and Dad got married, right?"

That's, of course, a massive oversimplification. Dad always said his love for my mom had sparked and combusted, burning hard and bright. His love for Uncle D had been embers, banked but glowing steadily for years. All the things they went through together—Mom's passing, raising two kids, starting and growing Uncle D's business— they were like adding logs to the embers, and soon enough, they had a steady, reliable fire going.

"So here's the secret," I say, leaning in. The room's quiet around me, everyone listening in to my so-called secret. "Uncle D actually means Uncle Dad now. A lot of people have stepdads in their lives, but no one has an Uncle Dad. Ours is very special, okay?"

They both nod, and Whitney reminds them to thank me.

"Hey, kiddos," Fritz calls from the tree. "I've got the railroad track done."

Molly leads the charge, and soon the kids are busy playing. I glance over at Uncle D, who's covering his mouth with his hands, his eyes glistening with unshed tears.

"Sugar Plum," Dad says softly, "that was so sweet."

Uncle D moves his hand, and he manages to choke out two words before the tears spill over. "Love you."

I lean into him, wrapping my arms around his waist. Uncle D and I have always shared a different connection than me with Dad or Uncle D with Fritz. The feel of his body, the tickle of his gray stubble against my cheek, is familiar and warm.

Whitney sniffs behind me, and when I turn around, she's wiping her eyes. "Sure, it's all cute when you have the back story, but when the kids tell their teacher they have an Uncle Dad, it's going to sound incestuous."

"Mom," Molly calls from where she's playing with her train. "What's incestuous?"

4

CLARA

"Okay, I'm going to head home, too," Nash says, and I rise to my feet, glancing at Uncle D and my dad. Fritz and his family left about an hour ago when the kids got too cranky. I think the parents were cranky, too, because Fritz argued that they should put the kids in bed here and stay longer, but Whitney said that waking the kids up in the middle of the night to move them back home would mean they were twice as irritable tomorrow.

It had been surprisingly hard to say goodbye to Fritz and his family. I knew I wasn't going to have time to see them again this trip, and I found myself wanting to side with Fritz. *Don't go yet.*

I'm not sure where that came from because, though I love my brother and his family, we haven't been super close.

I guess it's just the holiday season making me feel a little extra lonely. The four of us have been enjoying adult beverages—Uncle D sips cognac and the rest of us are drinking Madeira, a bottle I'd brought home after my trip to Portugal years ago that we never opened.

I glance at my dads. Dad looks mildly uncomfortable while Uncle D is trying hard to keep a neutral face.

Nash gives me a look and tilts his head toward the foyer leading to the elevator. I linger while he says his goodbyes and then we stand together at the elevator doors.

"Do you want me to come over?" The hope in my voice is nearly pathetic.

Nash shakes his head, and my stomach flips. What's happening? Is Nash changing our relationship now that Dad and Uncle D know? Or is he actually seeing someone? What if he wanted to tell me in person?

As if he can read it in my face, Nash comes forward and threads my fingers through his and pulls me close to him. "Hey," he says, and I look up into his rich brown eyes. "I get you all day tomorrow. Why don't you spend some time with your dad and Uncle Dad." His lips quirk up at the tease. "Be ready at eleven o'clock tomorrow, okay?"

"Okay."

A hand slips from mine and Nash touches my chin, tilting my head up to look at him. Our breaths mingle for a moment, and I think he's going to kiss me.

And he does. On the cheek. I try not to be too disappointed; try to understand, given that my parents are probably trying hard not to listen from the other room.

"Eleven o'clock," he reminds me.

I try to inject excitement into my voice. "See you then," I say. And then I tease him one last time. "Nutcracker!" I shout as the door closes, and Nash's laughter disappears.

———

THE FIRST THING I DO WHEN I WAKE UP IN THE MORNING IS check my emails.

Nothing.

Well, okay, not nothing. There are Boxing Day sales and a few corporate marketing Merry Christmas emails, but not the particular email I was hoping for, nor any fun emails from my globe-trotting friends.

I go limp in disappointment but remind myself that businesses are probably still closed for the holiday and my friends —most of them are online friends, people I've either met out traveling and have kept in touch with or other bloggers like myself—are probably visiting their own families or celebrating local Christmas traditions or sleeping off hangovers.

I force myself to roll out of bed. I'm in a tank top and underwear, so I should put something else on before exiting my room.

I send Nash a text.

Um, if today is a surprise, then what am I supposed to wear?

Nash's response is immediate. *What are you wearing now?* It's followed by a winking face, so Nash is in a flirty mood this morning.

I snap a selfie, sticking my tongue out, crossing my eyes, and throwing up a peace sign.

Sexy and perfect, he answers.

I send him an eye roll emoji, even though he actually made me smile and blush. This man does not need to know how much he affects me. *Seriously, Nash. What should I be wearing?*

I'm serious, Clara. Wear whatever you want. And be prepared to eat.

If only I could greet you at the door like this, I text back.

He sends me back a horny devil emoji.

I don't want to scandalize my dads, so I grab my pajamas from yesterday and throw on some of the fluffy socks that were in my stocking.

I hum to myself as I walk down the hallway. *Wear pajamas and be prepared to eat.* What could that be a hint for?

Uncle D and Dad's apartment is a far cry from how we grew up. My parents were high school sweethearts, married young, and had me and then Fritz. Money was always tight, especially after Mom died.

It was tight for Uncle D, too. Heartly was his third startup, and the first two had flopped. He likes to tell us stories of living on ramen and tutoring college kids, even though he didn't even have a college degree.

Dad and Uncle D have lived in this new place, a penthouse in Manhattan, for the last five years. The building itself is glassy and modern, but the home inside is warm. It's covered in pictures of our family. I walk down the hall past photos of the original four—Mom, Dad, me, and Fritz—and the new four, with Uncle D instead of my mom. But there are a few with all five of us back when mom was still alive. I stop in front of one of them, a picture of us at a Christmas party, Fritz on Dad's hip and me holding Mom's hand. I don't remember which company of Uncle D's this was, but the adults are dressed in cocktail attire and Fritz and I are in matching red velvet outfits. It's very cringe.

When I was five years old, my mom got diagnosed with cancer. I was too young to remember much, but the biggest memories of that time included Uncle D. He took care of Fritz and me when my parents were busy. To us, it was fun—Uncle D was Dad's best friend, and he quickly became ours. He was the one who introduced us to video games and rock music, and some of the best memories I have with Uncle D are complicated dichotomies—Fritz and I bouncing on Uncle D's couch in his apartment in Dover, screaming *A Horse with No Name* at the top of our lungs and then he would return us to my parents where we would hear Mom vomiting at night. Once, it was so bad Dad called the ambulance, and Uncle D came to pick us up in the middle of the night.

We started staying over at Uncle D's a lot more after that.

Until our time with Mom was spent in hospice.

I can hear the murmur of two low voices, so I pick up the

pace and slide into the great room, Risky-Business style, nearly knocking into a piece of art on the wall.

Dad's at the breakfast table, drinking coffee and reading the news on his tablet, but he glances up at me and rolls his eyes at my theatrics, trying not to laugh. "Our darling daughter has made an entrance," he says. Uncle D emerges from the pantry, an apron protecting his front that says *Sounds gay, I'm in*. "Morning, Sugar Plum."

"What? Hotels do not have the shiny floors nor the space for a running start. I *never* get to do this."

Dad squints at me. "I'm trying to remember if I was as energetic at your age. If I tried to do that now, I might break a hip."

"You aren't that old," I say, kissing him on his prickly cheek. "And when you were my age, you had kids. That ages you up, like, fifteen years." I do another small slide to come around the kitchen island, and Uncle D offers me his cheek, too.

"You hear that, Rolf? She just aged me up to seventy-nine."

I ignore my dad and sniff around the oven. "What are you baking?" I ask Uncle D.

"Cherry almond ricotta scones," he says.

I raise my eyebrows. "Plain ole scones not good enough for you?"

"I'm looking for a new challenge."

"You have too many hobbies. Last time I was here, you were cross-stitching curse words." There's one in my bathroom that says *Ahh . . . the fucks I don't give* with pink flowers and emerald vines.

"Rolf is afraid to be at loose ends," Dad says. "Ever since he cut back on his hours at the office, he's been picking up one hobby after another."

Uncle D's chest puffs up. "Semi-retirement keeps me busy."

I switch on the light inside the oven and bend over to look at the scones. "You had to bake these today? Nash says I should be prepared to eat when he gets me, which means I can't have a scone just yet."

"You can have coffee," Dad says and pours me a mug. We settle in catching up with each other, but I have a hard time focusing on the conversation. I keep wondering if this is when I'm finally going to lose Nash.

The first time Nash visited for a weekend my sophomore year, I took him to a party, and we were one of the last to leave, but instead of playing beer pong or flip cup or darts, and getting hammered like everyone else, we talked. We talked so much I was hoarse the next day.

It revealed a stark difference between him and other guys our age. Nash was serious and quiet. Broody, rather than verbose. He was more grown up than any of those dill holes, even the seniors.

My freshman year, missing Nash had been like missing my family. At the time, he was still living with his parents, and visiting me was entirely out of the question. They would never have allowed their son an unsupervised weekend with someone like me.

When he came to visit that sophomore year, something clicked. Nash was a different man. Sure, he was still quiet and serious, but he smiled more and he laughed more.

Over trash can punch, he opened up to me about living with his parents—the shouting matches, the hypocrisy, the anger that simmered. And he told me about moving in with my parents and how he'd tried to balance the two, but something had to give.

When Nash and I agreed to keep our benefits casual, there were plenty of good reasons, but the biggest one for me was that I would never live in New York City. And I knew, even when I first met Nash and he was still developing into the man he is today, that he would be a catch.

And I also knew that someday, if I let myself fall in love with him, he'd break my heart. Someday I'd come back home to find him in a relationship, and then I'd watch from afar while he fell in love. I'd fly back for his wedding, and I'd always see him and his wife because she'd become part of our family, too.

I would never regret sleeping with Nash. Our first time was awkward and gentle, but I trusted him with my body.

But I would regret falling in love with him.

5

CLARA

I HEAR DAD GREETING SOMEONE, AND WHEN I WALK AROUND THE corner into the foyer, it's not Nash coming in but Kara, his stylist. She's got a small clothing rack with her, hanging black bags swaying as she strides. She's got a rolling suitcase that clacks along the floor, too.

"Kara!" I shout and throw my arms around her.

"Clara!" She shouts back in the exact same tone, and we both giggle.

"What are you doing here?" I ask her, pulling back. It's been years since I've seen her, though, of course, I've kept up with her work—Nash always cuts a fine figure nowadays and Kara is one hundred percent responsible for that.

"Nash sent me to get you ready."

I roll my eyes at Nash for the second time today, even though we haven't even been in the same room yet. "I do have clothes with me."

"Honey, you know, I know, Nash knows—we all know! You pack light and for the tropics. You definitely do not have anything decent to tackle the winter here in the city."

I open my mouth to argue. I do keep some things here at Dad's place, like winter boots and pajamas.

"Nothing appropriate for today," Kara amends.

It's true. As much as I would love to visit lots of cold-weather places, packing light is more important for me. I have to carry a lot of gear—my cameras and laptop—plus plenty of outfits. Winter clothes are just too bulky.

I've always favored the tropics anyway. I'll take a beach-side cabana in a small town in Panama over a chalet in the Alps most days.

Though maybe not days when I could share that chalet with someone special . . .

Given that I have no idea where we're going either, I relent.

"Come on," Kara says, tugging my hand. "First we're doing hair, and then let's have you try on these dresses."

"Dresses?" I say, perking up. "Plural?" I let her lead me back to my room.

"Dresses," she confirms. Kara leads me to the en suite bathroom in my guest room. It's "small" compared to Uncle D and Dad's bathroom, but huge compared to what we grew up with. Between the his and hers sinks is a small vanity with a chair, and Kara pushes me down to sit.

"I'm going to give you something simple and elegant that will suit you all day, okay?" she says as she tugs at my hem. I raise my hands over my head as she pulls my T-shirt off so she can do my hair without messing it up when I change later. I'm in a simple nude bra and underwear set. Nash and I have been hooking up for so long that it started in simple under-things like this, and while I have *occasionally* surprised him with fancy underwear, usually, it's so impractical. I travel all the time—there's no sense in carrying around underwear that won't be comfortable while bouncing on a bus through Cambodia or cutting through jungles in Brazil.

And Nash always argues that he'd take me naked over anything else, so I don't miss fancy underwear at all.

Kara and I chat while she works, brushing my hair out and applying some product to it.

"How's your family?" I ask. Like Nash, Kara's family immigrated to the US but from Bulgaria. However, Kara's family is still close-knit; she lives with them in an apartment in the Bronx, last I checked. Kara is close to her family—really close. Like, they all lived together for *way* longer than most people I know. This especially surprised me because Kara is the opposite of the rest of her family. While her family is all in tech—her little sister even works at Heartly—Kara's decision to be a stylist went against the grain.

But Nash was one of her early clients, and now, especially since he's referred so many other clients to her, Kara can be picky on who she styles, and she often gets amazing opportunities because of it.

Just like with career choices, Kara's family has high standards when it comes to men their daughter can date, too.

When I ask about her dating life, she says she's just broken up with her boyfriend.

"We don't all have fabulous men like Nash sweeping us off to fabulous surprise dates. I can't wait to hear what you think of the activities today. Okay, that's your hair done."

I turn my head left and right. "It's a bun?" I say, a little surprised. My hair is twisted and tightly coiled in a low bun on the right side of my head.

"It's traditional for this afternoon. And practical enough for the rest of the day."

"That's cryptic. Traditional?"

"Don't worry about it. Now, dresses: I think this one is my favorite."

Kara unzips one of the hanging bags on the clothes rack and thumbs through the choices, flashing a variety of colors and textures at me before pulling out a pink dress. At first, I think she must be joking because it's understated, just a solid silk dress with a flared skirt and a simple and sleeveless high neckline.

But at closer look, the bodice is not so simple. Starting at the left shoulder is something like lace, but not a flowery pattern. It's geometric, almost a weave, and some of the material is tiny bands of silver. Some of the threads are missing, leaving seductive gaps in the dress where my pale skin will show through. This ribbon of silver and air travels across the breasts to taper off at the right side of the waist.

The skirt falls to my knees, flared out, and as Kara shifts the material, I see a hidden slit, much like the bodice, with gaps in the weaving that get progressively bigger as they move down toward the hem.

"It's gorgeous," I whisper.

Kara grins. "I know you like warm tones and something with an edge. I had to snag this for you when Nash told me his plans for the night."

She helps me into the dress, taking the bra when I peel it off and zipping up the back. I take my time, admiring the way the skirt flares and shimmers when I move. "This isn't too fancy for what we're doing tonight?"

"Nope," she says, popping the p with glee.

My eyes widen. Nash and I have always had fun, low-key days together, with the exception of galas for work. Today feels different. This dress . . . this is a to-kill-for dress, a Bond girl dress, a take-me-someplace-special dress.

"Wow. Okay, this dress it is."

Kara unzips a compartment in the suitcase. "Here's shoes." She holds out a pair of classic black peep-toes, my favorite style, but this pair is made to fit the dress, with silver threads running through it, too. Of course, she pulls out a faux-fur, full-length black coat to go with it. The shoes are comfortable, and the coat is warm.

I gaze longingly at myself before we undress me. I've dressed up like this maybe a dozen times, but it's still not something I'm used to. I think about Nash, with his business meetings and tailored suits, Kara dressing him frequently enough to be on retainer.

It's surreal how much our lives have changed.

Kara gives me a new bag of some of my favorite makeups and clothes for today, a black sweater, fitted jeans, and faux-fur-lined tall boots, perfect for a New York winter.

"You're going to do a lot of walking, and leggings and sneakers aren't going to keep you warm." She thrusts the clothes at me. "Put them on."

By the time I'm dressed, I also have a black wool coat "to go with everything," Kara says, plus ear muffs and gloves.

"Wow, we really are going to be outside a lot today," I remark. "Wait," I say as Kara starts to wheel the stand away with my dress for tonight. "Where are you going with the dress?"

"I'm delivering it to a spot where you'll have time to change this evening. Don't worry. I won't let anything happen to it."

"Okay. Bye, beautiful dress. I'll see you later." I stare at it longingly, and Kara giggles.

I walk out with her and find Nash in the living room talking to my dads.

"Hey," he says, rising when he sees me. "You look fantastic."

His arms slide around me, and he gives me a quick kiss on the cheek. It feels weird. Is this because I'm not used to PDA with him or because of the three people staring at us?

"Thanks," I say. "You look great, too. Are you ready to go?" I widen my eyes and tilt my head at our audience.

"Yup," Nash takes my hand. "You leaving, too, Kara?"

"Nah, Craig invited me for a coffee. I'll stay for a chat. You two have fun."

Nash and I, hand in hand, take off down the hall, ready to start our mysterious day of adventures.

6

NASH

"Where to first?" Clara asks as we step onto the street.

"Breakfast," I say.

"Thank goodness. Uncle D was baking scones, and it was torture." Clara rubs her gloved hands together in excitement. "Are we taking the subway, or are you too fancy for that?"

"It has nothing to do with being fancy. You haven't had your face on the cover of a magazine declaring you the most eligible bachelor." I nudge her. "We're taking the subway," I admit.

Clara eyes me. It's bright, so I'm wearing sunglasses, but I've got a beanie on, too. It's supposed to get overcast and chillier this afternoon, the temperature dropping into the evening, but for now, it'll help keep me blending in with the crowd.

She reaches over and pulls my beanie down and fusses with my scarf. I try to ignore the excitement that flares up when her fingers brush against my freshly-shaved face. "There, no one can tell it's you. I can hardly tell it's you. Don't wander too far, or we might get separated," she teases.

We step down into the nearest subway station and hustle onto the car.

"Did it feel weird for you yesterday? And this morning?" Clara asks as she grabs ahold of the pole.

"Weird how?"

"I mean, I wasn't going to tell my dads that we're friends with benefits, but now that they know, it feels like it puts pressure on us to act like we're more than that, don't you think?"

I frown in thought. "Do you feel pressured?"

"I think . . . " She trails off, frowning and biting her bottom lip.

The first few times we hooked up were clumsy and a little awkward. But I remember the first time I used my teeth, tugged a little harder on that bottom lip than I intended, and Clara let out a breathy moan. It felt like I'd unlocked the next level. I love unleashing my teeth on her now, and I know just how she likes to be nibbled.

Clara gives a small laugh, and I shake off the thoughts. "I tell myself that I'm a grown-up, and Dad always tried so hard to teach sex and body positivity, but there was always the feeling that he was uncomfortable. Sometimes I get these weird hang-ups, and I don't understand where they come from."

"It makes sense," I say. "Maybe trauma from your mom's death at such a young age, or just a side effect from growing up with few women around."

Clara's often confided in me that the feeling of loss hasn't ever gone away. She gets reminders all the time that her mom is gone.

While I don't think about it the same way, I get it. I get reminders all the time that my parents aren't a part of my life —a loss of a kind, but a different one.

Someone nearby giggles, and when I look up, there are two young women glancing at us. "I think I've been made," I stage-whisper to Clara, turning a little bit to put my back to them.

"Really?" She rises onto her tiptoes to peek over my shoulder. "It's like your disguise didn't work," she says dryly.

"Hush you."

"Oh, they're coming over."

"Well you *were* staring."

I plaster on a smile because, honestly, I only get so much time with Clara. I don't want interruptions.

The two women reach us and look at Clara. "We are so sorry to bother you," one of them says. I nearly roll my eyes. I can't believe they're going to ask Clara to take our picture without even asking me first. "But could we take a picture with you?"

My mouth drops open. The women haven't even looked at me.

"With me?" Clara asks, hand to her chest.

"Oh my god, yes," the other woman gushes. "We've been following your Instagram for years! I went to Recife last year because you raved about it. I am *such* a fan."

"Well, it is so nice to meet my followers." Clara rotates her head to stare at me, an amused look on her face. "I would love to take a picture. In fact, maybe my friend here could take one for us."

With barely a glance, I'm handed a phone. My cheeks are warm, and Clara is going to tease the hell out of me for this.

We take several pictures, the girls posing on either side of Clara. It's drawing some attention in the subway car, and I hear someone whisper my name.

"Okay, this is our stop," I say as we pull up to the station.

"It was so nice to meet you. Please post those photos and tag me, okay?" Clara gives each of them a quick hug before we weave through the crowd to the open door.

Wordlessly, we walk toward the exit as the doors close and the subway moves on.

Clara screeches to a halt. "Oh. My. God. That was hysterical!"

I hide my face in my hands, shoving my sunglasses up. "I can't believe that happened."

"You, sir, needed to be taken down a peg or two. Seriously, maybe that's why you need to take a car around town. Your ego doesn't even fit in the subway!"

She bends over, clutching her sides from laughing too hard.

There's no one on our side of the platform, and the people across the track are ignoring us as we lean against each other. Clara straightens, wiping tears from her eyes.

"I'm dying. That was too funny."

I shake my head, my face still too warm, my ears burning. "I'm never going to hear the end of this, am I?"

"No. I'll hold it over you for the rest of our lives."

And then, because I can't help myself, I lean over and kiss her. She's still laughing, so it's clunky, mostly kissing her teeth, but I do it anyway.

God, I love her.

Clara sobers, returning the kiss and cupping the back of my neck to keep me from pulling away. Her coat is open, so I slip my hand inside, splaying my fingers against her belly.

Which grumbles at me, vibrating against my skin.

We laugh again.

"Okay, let's go get some food," I say, pulling myself away from her and setting off to the exit.

A few minutes later, we arrive at the café, and I hold the door open for Clara. This one's a hole-in-the-wall, but I hear it's very good.

Clara doesn't mind appearances. I can take her anywhere, and she'll enjoy it, whether it's fluorescent lighting and old linoleum floors or the hottest new restaurant in the city.

"Two for breakfast, please," I tell the South Asian man behind the counter.

"Sit," he says, gesturing. There are ten tables in the whole place, and only two of them are unoccupied. Clara's the only white person in here.

The man from behind the counter brings us glasses of water.

"Where did you find this place?" Clara asks, looking around and slipping her coat onto the back of the chair.

"I can't reveal my secrets," I say. It took me longer than I would like to admit to plan this whole day. This particular place I found on a subreddit for Sri Lankans.

Her gaze returns to mine. "Will you at least tell me what we're eating?"

The place is pretty nondescript. "Breakfast."

She smacks my arm with the back of her hand. "Cheeky."

A waiter comes out from the kitchen and starts to set plates down in front of us.

"Oh, we didn't order these," Clara says.

The server freezes, glancing at me.

"It's fine, yeah."

The plate, oblong and China-white with dozens of years' worth of scratches on it, clacks on the table as he sets it down. Our plates are followed by small bowls for the center of the table, bright red and fragrant.

"Sambal," the server says, pointing. "Kiri hodi and dal."

Each plate has two bowl-shaped items on it, and each bowl has a cooked egg in the center.

"There's only one thing on the menu for breakfast here," I explain. "This is called an egg hopper."

Clara pokes at one of hers with her fork. "Is this . . . oh, it's a batter, like a pancake! It's a pancake bowl!"

She grins in amazement and pokes the lacy edges of the bowl again. Then her attention moves to the small dishes in the center. Clara dips her fork in each one, bringing it to her lips and tasting the condiments.

"Ho boy," she says, and fans her mouth, sticking out her tongue. "Tha ones 'ot."

Nevertheless, Clara takes a big scoop of the condiment and plops it onto her egg hopper. Then she turns her fork to the side and uses the edge to cut the battered bowl.

"Wait—" I say, and Clara freezes, her fork hovering, posed to make a second cut. "Aren't you going to take pictures?"

"Pictures?"

"Yeah. For your blog or Instagram."

"Oh." She pulls back her fork. "I was planning on taking today off. You know, be present with you."

I deflate a little bit. "Oh, yeah. I mean, that makes sense." Never mind that I had pictured her capturing everything I'd planned for today and sharing it over the next few weeks. I would look at her profile every day—which, let's be honest, I do already—and I would see photos from *our* adventures together. I'll get these little reminders of the day spaced out like a morphine drip.

Clara must see something in my face because she laughs and reaches into her purse. "No, you're right. I can never have too much content."

She whips out her camera and snaps some pictures, moving both our plates around and then doing close-ups of the condiments.

If life continues on as is, Clara will disappear to some new corner of the world, and I'll be stuck looking at her life through a lens. Maybe it'll just be a few photos, or maybe she'll write a blog post about today.

Five Unique Foods You Must Try in New York.

Skip the Flight: Five Places to Eat in New York to Save Your Vacation Days.

Five Foods I'd Never Tried Before.

But maybe, this time, something will change.

After thirty, forty, maybe even fifty photos, Clara puts her phone away.

"Permission to eat now?" she asks with a grin.

"Permission granted."

We both dig in.

"So," Clara begins with a glance up at me from under her eyelashes. She fiddles with her fork, pushing some dal around the plate. "Did you break up with someone recently?"

My brows draw together. "No?"

Clara uses the side of her fork to cut into the egg yolk. "In the article, you said there was someone special."

"You think I was dating someone? Come on, you'd definitely know about it." It surprises me that Clara thinks I wouldn't tell her. We message frequently, no matter where she is in the world, and besides, if I was publicly dating someone, I feel pretty confident that she would tease me about the media circus that would follow.

That's replaced by a pang of guilt. I had been too busy leading up to the holidays, and I guess it had slipped my mind to assure her that I was still single, just like I wasn't going to stay with Craig and Rolf. I should have told her that I was excited to see her like I always am.

Like the rest of Clara's family, she's always been down-to-earth and definitely not interested in what the gossip columns have to say. They have mostly kept out of the news—Clara's never here, and Fritz leads his unassuming life with his family. The media didn't even get to splash Uncle D's sexuality in people's faces—he was publicly gay long before the company grew into the juggernaut that it is today.

But I can't keep out of the media. Our PR firm says it's a good thing, but I find it exhausting and detracting from my real work.

Clara shrugs. "I just can't understand how you're still single, sometimes."

I open my mouth to answer but my phone pings. It's set on do not disturb for the day, so the only reason it's pinging is that there's a message from one of the select few people that I want to hear from on this day off—Kara, Craig, Uncle D, or my assistant, Bea.

The message is from Kara, in the group text between me, her, and Bea. *Just left Rolf's. How's the first stop?*

Immediately a message comes in from Bea. *Squeee! I want updates!*

I type out a quick *tasty so far, thanks for all the help*. Bea and Kara have both been helping me plan—Bea as my assistant, and Kara because she's been rooting for me and Clara since the day she found out about us. It only took her picking up my tuxes and Clara's dresses twice the morning after galas before she put two and two together.

Clara diverts our conversation back to the food, and we finish off our plates. I pay, and we walk out of the café, feeling satisfied but not full.

"You know I could pay for these things and expense them, right?" Clara remarks.

"Absolutely not," I say, putting my hand on her lower back and steering her to the left. Our next stop isn't far.

"Why, because you're a man?" she teases. "Or because you're a billionaire."

I roll my eyes. "I'm not a billionaire."

"An almost-billionaire."

We bicker like this until we reach our destination. I know it's coming, so I can smell the coffee from two blocks away.

"Oh man," Clara says, head turning as we walk past the door. "That place smells amazing."

I gently guide her into the next alleyway.

"Nash," she says, mock-affronted. "Are you pulling me in here to have your wicked way with me?"

I laugh. "Later. For now, we're at our next stop."

Clara glances back over her shoulder and then to the door a few steps in front of us. "Is this the same place? The place that smells so good?"

There's a sign to the left that says, "by appointment only." I knock. "It is."

Clara claps her hands in glee and the door opens.

"Nash, welcome." Freddy offers me his hand and I take it. We haven't met before, or even talked on the phone, but Bea made all the arrangements, so he knew to expect us. Freddy is tall and lean, with shaggy blonde hair and a wide smile. "And you must be Clara," he says, offering her his hand.

"Clara, this is Freddy Soren. This is his café."

"Nice to meet you, Freddy," she says.

"Come in, come in." He waves us in and leads us immediately to the right, where there's a small, brightly lit room. "This is our tasting room. Have a seat, and I'll be back in a few minutes to get started."

There's a couch and coffee table with two upholstered chairs across from it. Clara peels her coat off and tosses it over the arm of the couch before settling into the corner, crossing her legs. "What are we tasting?"

I put my jacket over the back and just smile and shrug at her.

"God, Nash," she says. "So secretive." But she says it with a small smile, so I know she's enjoying herself.

"Here we are," Freddy says from the doorway, and he's followed by two of his staff carrying long, white trays. A tray is set down in front of each of us.

Clara peers down at the four small espresso cups in front of her. "Smells fantastic. Do you mind if I take pictures?"

"Go ahead. Each cup is a brew of a different type of coffee bean," Freddy explains, perching on a chair across from us. "Most coffee drinkers know the two major ones, Arabica and Robusta. But there are two more: Liberica and Excelsa. What we do here is very small batches of the last two, exclusively for our tastings. These beans are much harder to get, so we don't serve them publicly. What kind of coffee do you usually drink?" he asks.

"I actually don't know," Clara says. "I usually just get whatever is available, and it's not always consistent."

"What about you?" Freddy asks me.

"I drink Arabica," I answer. I only know because I checked the bag in my kitchen.

"We'll start with that one then." Freddy instructs us to take one cup—the second from the left—and sit back on the couch and focus on the smell and taste.

"I try my best to roast and brew the beans as similarly as possible, but because they have different properties, it doesn't always work. Brewing a more exotic bean the same way you would brew an Arabica makes it bitter and is part of the reason why the rare beans haven't caught on as well."

"You know, I have been to tea rooms before, where there's a giant menu of teas from around the world—white, green, black, etcetera," Clara says, "but I don't think I've ever heard of such a variety of coffee tastings."

"There's a lot of variety in tea, in terms of the base leaves, but there are rare and delicate tea types, too, that you won't get at most tea rooms," Freddy explains. "And just like coffee beans, some of them are cost prohibitive."

"Like that civet coffee?" Clara asks, a teasing smile on her lips.

Freddy laughs and rolls his eyes. "We went through a phase where at least every day someone was asking for civet-poop coffee."

"Did you serve it?" I ask. I remember hearing about it and thinking it was like gold-leafing a burger—it probably didn't taste that great, and it was mostly for looks and prestige.

Freddy shakes his head. "That coffee is produced in places like Indonesia that have problematic treatment of animals and a lack of a system in place to regulate it. I'm too picky with my social mores to sell it. Try the coffee now."

Clara and I sip. It's familiar, a dark roast with a hint of sweetness. A baseline.

It's only a few sips and the mug is empty. Freddy has us cleanse our palettes with sparkling water, and we move through the rest of the cups.

Clara is much better at this than I am. She asks Freddy questions about the beans, how he got into serving such a variety of coffees and when he opened his café. She also blooms under his attention like a teacher's pet—they bond over her ability to sense the different profiles.

It reminds me that this is Clara's way of reconnecting with her mom. On her blog and in interviews, Clara talks about how she got into travel: one day, with Craig, they were going through some of her mom's things and discovered a blank passport. When Clara saw who it belonged to, she asked why it had never been used.

Craig and Deb had married young and never got a honeymoon. First, there was no money, and then they were pregnant with Clara.

Deb's first passport had come in the mail days prior to her abnormal pap smear. The trip was postponed, there was testing and attempts to treat the cancer.

But that trip never got taken.

It surprised no one when months after finding the passport, Clara announced she wanted to travel the world for a living.

Clara believes it's one of her dad's deepest regrets that he never took her mom on a vacation. So Clara makes up for it by carrying her mom with her all over the world.

As much as I hate that it takes Clara away from me, I'm so proud of her, and I know she needs to feel that connection to the mom she lost when she was so young.

I'm happy to listen while Freddy and Clara discuss the coffees, and then he asks which is her favorite.

"The Liberica," she says quickly. "I like the fruitiness. How much do those beans cost compared to the others?"

Clara blanches when Freddy gives her the numbers. I nudge her. "Good thing you aren't paying."

Clara sticks out her tongue.

"I'll bring you a to-go cup in a few minutes." He picks up both platters and leaves.

"That was so interesting. Freddy is super knowledgeable," she says, leaning back against the couch.

"Glad you enjoyed it."

"You know that I toured a coffee farm in Brazil once, right?"

"I do."

"I don't even remember what type of bean it was, but I would guess I wrote it down somewhere. I actually have plans to go to another coffee farm in Indonesia while I'm there. Not a civet one, thank god."

I cross an ankle over my knee, getting comfortable, and stretch an arm out over the back of the couch. "Is that where you are headed next?"

"Yup. I have New Year's Eve in Sydney and then two months booked out between Australia, Indonesia, Singapore, and Malaysia."

"Why there?"

"I have a few partners I'm working with in Australia, and then Indonesia and Malaysia are cheap and there's a big expat community. It's summer down there, so I'll be comfortable leaving my winter gear behind." She plucks at the coat next to her. "But there's so much to do, and travel is cheap in South-east Asia. I wouldn't be doing Australia because it's too expensive, but I worked out a deal with an airline there and picked up a few sponsorships."

"So, you have big New Year's Eve plans?"

"Argh." Clara slumps against the couch. "When I'd booked my flight to Sydney, I reached out to a bunch of companies, and one of them emailed me back last week, saying they had a cancellation on a media ticket for their New Year's Eve event. I emailed back right away, but I haven't heard anything. I wonder if I should even go, honestly, or if I should save it for next year. All the parties are sold out."

Hope flutters in my chest, followed immediately by guilt. I'd love more than anything to have Clara stay here for New Year's Eve. But if she wants a New Year's Eve party in Sydney, then she should be at a New Year's Eve party in Sydney.

My feelings are complicated, okay?

"You could stay here. I'm ninety-nine percent certain you haven't written an article on the best places to watch the fireworks in New York."

She grins at me. "First of all, my article would have to be the best *public* places to watch the fireworks, and Uncle D and Dad's apartment doesn't count."

Well, I had been thinking about my apartment, preferably naked in bed with a bottle of champagne, but okay.

"Secondly, you know my motto . . . " she trails off, expecting me to fill in the blank.

I obey. "Everywhere is worth going."

"Yeah." She sighs. I remember when she came up with the name for her blog. She was in college, planning a trip to Europe for the first time, and she was dumbstruck by people asking if a place was *worth going to*. "Every place is worth going to. Even if the trip is horrible, you go somewhere, meet new people, explore new places. You learn what *not* to do. Even a bad trip is a trip worth having," she'd said.

Perhaps she had been naive at the time, but her attitude held out. Clara's so positive and optimistic. She makes the best of anything.

And the name of her blog, *Worth Going*, suits her perfectly.

"Here you go," Freddy says as he enters the room carrying two paper cups of coffee. The name of his shop, *Bean Water*, is printed on the sleeve. We thank Freddy for his time and step out onto the street. Clara holds out her cup and snaps a photo of it, the café facade blurred out behind it.

"Nice business," she comments, and I expect that *Bean*

Water will get some positive publicity in a few days. She pockets her phone and turns back to me. "Where to next?"

"Brooklyn."

She raises an eyebrow at me. "What's there?"

"You'll see," I say.

We take the subway again. I check my phone and send a quick message to Bea. *Liberica is her favorite.*

When we exit the station, the streets are much busier. I take Clara's hand, and we weave through the crowd of people and into a building a few blocks later.

Clara takes a deep inhale. "It smells amazing again! But not coffee?"

The hallway opens into a vast, multi-leveled room, and Clara discovers the answer to her own question. "A spice market!"

Piles of spices in all shades of brown, beige, tan, or even brighter colors like orange, red, yellow, and green line the walkways. It's an eclectic mix of Middle Eastern cultures, with flags proudly displayed representing many different countries.

"Some of these vendors make their own proprietary spice blend," I say. "I figured that the smallest pouch or two might fit into your luggage. And you could buy something for your family. Maybe a gift for your dad?"

One thing about Clara is how *good* she is at traveling and meeting people. All our lives, she's been this gregarious person, the kind who's never met someone they couldn't befriend. We met up in Tokyo once when I was there for work, and while dining at a sidewalk bar, Clara struck up a conversation with the businessmen next to us. Next thing I know, we're at a karaoke bar downing Asahi beer with these men, and Clara and I are belting out *Hard Day's Night*.

Now I watch her talking with the people who work at the spice stalls, asking them questions and getting permission to take pictures. Sometimes, they try to engage me, but my

Arabic is rusty and clunky on my tongue now, a bitterness I'd rather not taste.

After an hour, we depart with five small satchels of spices. I have no idea what they are, but Clara tucks them into her bag, and we walk away, the scent of spices lingering on our clothes.

Our next stop is back in Manhattan.

Clara lets me lead as we cut through Central Park. We're right on time, and a crowd has gathered for the performance.

In the center is a slim white man with graying hair and a goatee. He's dressed in a loose top, striped, belted pants, and soft black leather boots. I've seen him perform before, so I'm familiar with the setup: a slightly raised floor, speakers, and his clapboard that reads: *I danced for Russia, Russia hunted me*, with a pride flag painted next to it. There's a bucket with a slotted lid and the logo of an organization that provides legal aid to LGBTQIA+ Russians.

The dancer, Ioann, claps his hands together, the final touches on his stage done. Ioann has done all sorts of ballet performances, from *Swan Lake* to his own choreography of Taylor Swift. I used to see him pretty regularly when I lived with Uncle D and walked to our office, but he hadn't achieved his TikTok notoriety yet.

With a press of a button, "A Mad Russian's Christmas" is off to an energetic start. Ioann spreads his arms, tilts his head back, and launches himself into the air.

I spend half the time watching Ioann, half watching Clara. The performance is energetic, and Clara gasps with each acrobatic feat. At the crescendo, Ioann leaps, hanging in the air, his body fully rotating around one stationary leg before he lands. Then he does it again and again and again.

"That's called a barrel turn," I say. Yeah, I'm showing off my knowledge.

Clara shoots me a surprised look, but the music builds, drawing our attention back.

The grand finale is a pirouette, Ioann spinning in place, tighter and tighter, his head stationary, a feat I'm not sure how he manages on a makeshift stage in Central Park, but he does, and the crowd cheers and screams as it goes on for longer than should be possible. Finally, with a flourish, both musical and physical, Ioann stops on one knee, a hand on his hip and his other in the air, with a beaming smile on his face.

Clara and I clap with the masses, people whistling and shouting as Ioann rises to his feet and takes a bow.

"That was amazing," Clara shouts over the noise. We shuffle with the crowd toward the donation collection and talk about the strength and physics required to perform the stunts. My phone dings and I slip it out to check.

How was Ioann? Kara texts. *If you get to talk to him, tell him I said hello. I still can't believe his only requirement for putting on a show the day after Christmas was to make a big donation. What a sweetheart.*

He's busy with adoring fans and we have a schedule to keep, I text back.

True. I just left Nikita's. Have a great lesson!

Bea chimes in. *I called Nikita to make sure she's going to get some pics or a video of you two dancing.*

Thanks! I respond.

While I put my phone away, Clara slips a bill out of her wallet, and even though I told her I would pay for everything, I let this one slide.

I take a hundred-dollar bill out of my own wallet and slip it into the can.

7

CLARA

"WHAT ARE YOU THINKING ABOUT?" NASH ASKS. WE'VE BEEN walking quietly through Central Park, Nash guiding us in the right direction.

I sigh. "Ethics," I tell him.

"Oh, so nothing important then?" he teases.

I smile, chagrined. "I know. Sorry. Seeing his sign," I gesture back toward the Russian dancer, "just made me think about some things. Like, I would love to go to Russia because it's such a unique place. But obviously, there are some problems with it. And where do I draw the line?"

Nash nods. "It is complicated."

"Freddy mentioned the ethics of the civet coffee in Indonesia, and I know there are other problems there, but I'm still going. There are problems with every place, too. Even home has problems that make me nervous."

"Like what?"

"Well, I've gotten medical care all over the world whenever I've needed it. And so many times the care has been very good, with doctors trained in the US or UK. And it's *way* cheaper. I basically come here and hope nothing happens to me. And I am lucky enough to be able to afford it if something does happen. But being uninsured in the United States is scary."

Nash hums next to me.

"Anyway, the point is that I was thinking about deep, important questions that probably aren't setting the mood well for our day of adventures." I smile up at Nash. "Let's talk about something else, okay?"

He wraps an arm around my shoulder. "Don't get me wrong, I love having fun with you, but I like these deep discussions, too. It reminds me of when we were teenagers and talking about my parents."

I lean into Nash. Those were some long and deep conversations. While I talked with the rest of my friends about boys or music or summer vacations, Nash and I were talking about conservative religions and emancipation and the right for queer people to marry.

"I enjoy talking to you about deep things, too."

"But," Nash says, nudging me, and I lift myself back up, "it's the day after Christmas and we're in one of the greatest cities in the world where we could do almost anything we want to. Including," Nash stops at a carved wooden door, grabbing the handle and pulling it open for me. It's a nondescript apartment building, and we're still in Manhattan, so it's a *nice* one. "Dancing."

"What? We're going dancing?"

Nash tips his head toward the building. "Come on."

We ride a fancy elevator up and then walk down the hallway, where Nash knocks on a door.

It swings open, revealing that last person I expected to see; Nikita Howley, the dancer from that reality show.

"Nash," she says, opening her arms to welcome him in a hug and kiss his cheek. The familiarness sparks some jealousy from out of nowhere, and I tamp it down. "Early, as always.

And hello." Nikita turns her attention to me. "You must be Clara. So nice to meet you."

While I hadn't watched *Dancing with the Stars*, I know who Nikita is. She's been on the show for years and is an expert in tango, having been born in Argentina and danced professionally her whole life.

We shake hands. "Nice to meet you, too," I say.

"Come in, please." Nikita waves us in. Her accent is thick and rich, and she's dressed to dance in a black dress that clings and is short enough to reveal muscular thighs. It's got an asymmetrical train that dangles down and whips around as she guides us through the entryway and into a dance studio. I notice that her hair is in a tight bun just behind her right ear, like mine.

"Are we really dancing?" I ask.

"Ah, don't say it with so much fear, darling," Nikita says. "You are in good hands with Nash." She pats his chest, and . . . did Nash just lean into it? "Kara dropped off your clothes, so Clara you are in this room and Nash in the one next to it." She points at the two doors off to the side. "You'll find everything you need, but shout if you need help."

Bewildered, I glance at Nash, who's grinning.

"What have you gotten me into?"

"I think it's you who's gotten us into this, really."

I snort, pushing the door open. It's a bathroom, but a really nice one. There's a chaise lounge and hooks on the walls for clothes, and it's all a lush red with gold trim. It even smells good, lightly floral, and there's a full-length mirror and a toilet.

Two black garment bags hang from one of the hooks and, like Alice in Wonderland, Kara has marked one of them as "Open Me First." I do, and inside is a dress similar to Nikita's but royal blue. The train is a little different, and while Nikita's was strappy, mine has a one-shouldered long-sleeve top.

When I exit the room, in my dress and black dancing shoes—sturdy heels with a strap at the ankle—Nash is already out chatting with Nikita. I feel that sharp envy coil in my belly again. They obviously know each other and have repartee. They look good together.

And, well, she lives here, in the city, not far from Nash's apartment.

And the article said . . .

I shake that thought out of my head. You can't believe everything you read.

When my door clicks shut, Nash turns to me, and suddenly, I'm not jealous. His gaze meanders down my body over the tight dress, the length of my legs. It's cold in here, but when Nash's eyes come back to mine, they burn.

Nikita claps briskly. "Clara." She strides over and clasps my cheeks. "Perfection. Now, Nash and I will demonstrate."

Nash and Nikita face each other and Nash transforms. His posture straightens, he steps carefully up to Nikita, and they embrace, Nash's right arm around her back, high, his hand a few inches away from some side boob. His left hand cups her right, holding it up, their chests close together.

"Now, we learn the basic step. One, two, three . . . "

With each count, Nash and her step together, slowly and carefully, around the room. After a few counts of eight, Nikita stops counting out loud and starts talking to me about what her feet are doing.

It's hard to focus on her feet, especially when I catch sight of Nash's face. During the coffee tasting, he did a lot of smiling and nodding, but I gathered that a lot of the nuanced flavors were out of reach.

Here, Nash moves confidently, comfortably. He looks like he's enjoying himself, which is ironic because I'm slightly terrified.

"Now, your turn," Nikita says.

"Oh, I haven't really been—"

"Do not worry. This is part of the dance. You try it, and with a good partner like Nash, you will catch on quickly. And today, it's just for fun. I won't be so serious about technique. We just have a good time, okay?"

Here goes nothing, I think and square my shoulders. Nikita and I stand together, and she walks me through the steps. The first one isn't so bad—a step to the side, I can handle—but then it gets complicated with what Nikita calls a cruzada—a cross step—and I flub it a few times.

After the fifth flub, Nikita tells me it's time to dance with Nash.

"This is the beauty of dancing. You will make mistakes, you will stumble, but your partner will be right here waiting for you. You come back to him every time."

Nash grins, I'm not sure if it's because of my discomfort or in spite of it, but he takes my right hand and wraps his arm around me, just like he did with Nikita.

We walk through the steps, which I occasionally forget, but just like Nikita says, Nash is always there, ready to start again.

He's so freaking patient with me.

The first time I nail the eight-count movement, Nikita bursts into applause, and I blush.

"Not so bad, right?" Nash says, his voice low with a hint of pride.

We do it three more times and then Nikita stops us. "Next move: the ocho."

This step is *way* easier. It's a step and rotate, step and rotate. "We couldn't learn this one first?" I grumble.

Nikita teaches us more complicated moves, adornos—embellishments—and combined with the confidence of the basic steps, the feel of Nash's body next to mine, his eyes watching my movements, it's more fun—and sexy as hell.

With a move called a caricias, I sweep one leg against the other. Nikita tells me to pay attention to Nash's body, to watch his shoulders, feel his hips.

"The last thing I will teach you is the dip. Very sexy, you will like."

Nikita and Nash show me the position, how we slide our legs out together and then I hook my leg over his. At first, it's awkward, but then we practice and smooth it out.

"And then," Nikita says, "you trust Nash. Feel his strength and his energy pushing you."

We take the steps again. Five, six, seven, eight, and there is no one I trust more in the world than Nash, so I let myself go. My back arches over his arm, our hips still snapped together.

"Very good. And now, with the music."

We do the routine from the top, taking the simple steps. I fudge a caricias or two, but Nash pulls it back together, and we get to the dip. The world is upside-down as the song comes to a dramatic end, and all I can see is our reflection in the mirror. Even upside-down, I can admire Nash's focus, his concentration.

Then he looks up into the mirror, too, and smiles at me. It lights me up inside in a way I've never experienced before.

Slowly, Nash pulls me upright, my chest against his, his lips just at my line of sight. He still feels solid, like I could rely on him to be there. Anywhere I want to go, Nash will follow me.

With a sinking heart, I realize that's not the way it is, and it's not really what I want. It never will be what I want. Nash is his own man, with his own successes. He's powerful. He's stable.

He can't follow me.

But tonight, I can follow him. Nash's chest heaves against mine, my leg is around his hip, and I can feel his cock against me. His lips are right there. I want to kiss him and drag him back to his place and spend every last moment there until my flight.

As if reading my mind, Nash's eyes are hooded and lusty. His lips part.

Clapping sounds, and Nash and I both blink. I'd completely forgotten that Nikita was here.

8

NASH

"Bravo," Nikita claps, approaching us from the corner where she'd been watching. Clara startles, breaking our eye contact.

"You both did wonderfully. I told you he was a very good dancer, no?" Nikita nudges Clara with her elbow. I release Clara's hand and take a step back.

"He is very good," Clara says, laughter glimmering in her eyes when we glance at each other.

I enjoy dancing with Nikita, and those lessons all paid off. I felt confident, comfortable holding Clara, teaching her the dance and guiding her.

But dancing with her was a whole other level. Nikita is sexy—I'd be lying if I denied it—but she's not the one I want.

Clara is. And feeling her fall into my arms like that, feeling her trust me, the way our bodies talked and touched, lit me up inside.

None of our moves were particularly sexy, except for the dip, which presses our lower bodies together, but it was *fun*. It was work, too, and while the studio is kept chilly, my arms are shaky. I hope Clara didn't feel it.

"Your time is up, but I do hope you'll come for another

lesson on your next visit, Clara. But for tonight, Bea will have my hide if I do not get you two out the door on time."

She gestures to the bathroom. "Go change. Chop, chop."

About ten seconds after I close the door behind me, there's a knock. I've barely unbuttoned my shirt, so I call out, "Come in."

Clara slips into the room. "Hi," she says, and when I turn to face her, she presses her palms against my stomach, sliding them up to my chest.

"You've got horny eyes," I tell her.

"So do you," she whispers, her lips finding my chin and planting an open kiss on it. Her hands run back down and tuck under my belt. "We can be quick. I already took my panties off."

I close my eyes and take a deep breath in. It's supposed to be calming, but I swear I can smell her arousal.

Clara and I are used to fast and urgent. One time, Uncle D threw a New Year's Eve party, and we fucked our way into the new year in the guest bathroom. She had an early flight that morning, so time was of the essence. On longer visits, Clara is impatient and needy at first, but once I get her off, she's soft and pliant and tender.

I can't decide which I like more.

But I can never say no to Clara.

I push her hands off my belt and press her against the door. "It has to be really quick." My hands are already trailing up the inside of her thigh.

Her breath hitches. "Or we can skip dinner and pick up Shake Shack."

"Trust me," I say, nipping her bottom lip. "You want to go to this dinner." That and Bea would *absolutely kill* me if we didn't make it. Getting a seat at this restaurant is hard, even if you just had your face on the cover of a magazine.

There's a patch of dampness on her thigh inches below her cunt, and I moan in her ear when I hit it. I tease her, circling my finger even though I know we don't really have time for this.

"It's a good thing," Clara says, then gasps as I trace her seam. She has to catch her breath before she can continue. "It's a good thing it's been ten months, fifteen days, and I don't know . . . a few hours since I've been with anyone else?"

That was . . . that was me. She hasn't been with anyone since we were last together?

I do quick math. "Ten months, fifteen days, two hours, and fifteen minutes since you've been with anyone else. Give or take."

Clara laughs, but it's pained as I circle her clit. My two fingers are slick and she's swollen, easy to find. I press harder, and she grabs my biceps, fingers digging in.

"I'm so close already," she warns.

"Just to take the edge off. I'll take good care of you later."

"I know. I know, I know, I know . . . " Clara's babbling stops, and her mouth falls open on a silent scream. She's on the tips of her toes. I can feel her pulsing and wish that I was buried inside of her.

Instead, I let her come down and pull my hand out from under her skirt, sticking my fingers in my mouth and sucking her juices off.

Clara's head falls back. "God, I needed that."

I step back and adjust her dress. "Go change. You're going to make us late."

Her chest rises with a big sigh, and she pushes herself off the wall. As she steps through the door, I pinch her butt, making her yelp and laugh.

"We can't be late!" I call.

Fifteen minutes later, Clara emerges in the dress Kara picked out for her: pink and bright and shimmering between the lapels of her coat; perfectly Clara. She's reapplied her makeup, a little heavier this time. Her legs are smooth and long in her heels, her cheeks flushed, whether from my perusal or from the orgasm I gave her, I can't tell.

I love Clara any way she comes, whether it's wonky Christmas pajamas or yoga pants and tank tops. But there's something about seeing her dressed up in clothes I bought her . . .

I think it's the best benefit of my wealth.

Well . . . behind all the good causes I can support.

I offer her an arm. "Ready?"

"Our stuff?" She gestures back into her room, where everything is neatly packed up.

"Kara will come get it."

We ride the elevator back down, and when we emerge from the building, there's a black sedan waiting for us in the dark evening.

"Oh, now we're really fancy. Snubbing-our-nose-at-the-subway fancy."

"Oh, hush you," I say, opening the car door for her. "It's cold, and you've got heels on. Allow me the indulgence."

Once Clara's scooted to the other side, I climb in, shut the door, and give the driver a nod.

"I noticed something about today," Clara starts as we pull away from the curb.

"Yeah?" I adjust my coat and set my hand on the seat between us, wiggling my fingers. "What did you notice?"

Street lights pass outside the window, shadows rolling over Clara's face. My heart beats faster while I wait for her to twine our fingers together . . . or for her to catch on to my plan.

"I've never been to Sri Lanka." She lets her palm glide against mine and then taps the tips of our fingers together.

"You haven't."

"I haven't been to Colombia either. Or Russia, or Morocco, or Argentina."

She smiles at me, and I say nothing, my heart beating

faster, her hand soft and delicate in mine. The whole day has been built around Clara seeing that she can taste all these places she's never been to right here in the city. I've brought her to them, all without leaving the five boroughs.

"I think it's pretty clever. Making me excited to visit all these places, giving me a taste of something I'll experience for real someday."

My smile slips until I paste it back on. "Oh?"

"Yeah. And I wonder what we're going to preview next."

9

CLARA

I TAP MY CHIN, PRETENDING TO THINK. "I'M PICTURING A VENN diagram. It's got to be an overlap of places I've never been, places I want to go, and places you can experience the culture in New York."

In my coat pocket, my phone buzzes. I shift to the side, toward Nash, to pull it out.

"Antarctica?" I say, teasing him. I glance down at my phone, and my heart skips a beat at the notification. It's an email from the cruise company I've been talking to about the trip to Sydney. The email I've been waiting for all week.

My eyes widen as I tap on the notification.

"What is it?" Nash asks, leaning toward me.

"Hang on, hang on." I scan the email. My contact, Jess, apologizes for taking so long to get back to me, but if I'm still coming to Sydney, the pass is mine. "Oh my god, I got the trip! I'm going to be on the harbor for New Year's Eve. On a freaking boat!"

I squirm with excitement in my seat. Nash is on the other side of the car, a little too far for an enthusiastic hug, but he's watching me. I don't think he gets how truly awesome this chance is for my business because he's smiling, but it's mildly amused and a little . . . sad, maybe?

"I know this seems ridiculous to be excited about being on a yacht for New Year's. I'm sure you have friends that have yachts, right? Or do you have a yacht? Maybe you've been hiding a hundred-foot super yacht from me," I muse.

He laughs. "No, I don't have a yacht. Tell me why this is so big for you?"

I hug my phone to my chest, my fingers pressing against the silver woven lace at the top.

"First of all, it's a big company, and this is a small event, but I hope it'll open the door for me to work with them. They have small ship cruises all over the world, and I am dying to go on one. I want to kick ass with them, show them how much I can do in a partnership. I'm trying to get more involved with all-inclusive packages. It's less work for me to organize my trips this way. And, this company, despite being a cruise liner, is completely food-focused."

My blog combines my two loves: food and travel. I wanted to know about making real balsamic vinegar or how caviar was harvested, and that's what my followers want to know, too. Based on my business plan, I build my blog around my niche: culinary travel.

"They have shore excursions centered around food. There's one they do in Tasmania where you learn how to harvest shellfish and then learn how to shuck and prepare them around a beach bonfire. And another where they visit Nordic seaside villages in the arctic and learn how to smoke fish."

"What's the food theme for the Sydney cruise?" Nash asks.

"Australian native flavors. It's a bit general for the New Year's Eve cruise," I admit. "But it's still a foot in the door. This company meshes so well with everything I do. Honestly, if I'd known it existed, maybe I would have tried to get a job there."

Nash leans closer to me. "Instead of your blog?"

"Yeah, I guess. But it would have been a completely different path. I would have been working with customers and on someone else's schedule."

Our car pulls to the curb and stops. I glance out the window, and there's a bright red door softly lit with a back-lit sign with Asian characters. There isn't an English translation, so I'm still wondering where we are.

The driver comes around to open my door.

"This is where we're going?" I ask, standing on the sidewalk as Nash slips out behind me. "Is that Chinese?"

"Yes." Nash puts his hand on my lower back, guiding me toward the door.

"Oh wait, hang on." There's not much pedestrian traffic, but I pull over to the side anyway. "Can I answer this email real quick?"

I've already got my phone out and unlocked.

"Sure," Nash says and leans against the wall next to me.

Jess,

Thank you so much for the opportunity. I am very excited to be working with you and look forward to the cruise.

I tap send, and my email whooshes halfway around the world. I take a moment to squeeze my eyes closed, mentally fist pumping in excitement.

"Okay," I say, and open my eyes. "I'm ready for dinner. But, Nash, I have to tell you, you've made a fatal mistake." I cluck my tongue and shake my head disparagingly as he opens the door for me.

"What's that?"

"I've been to China before."

Nash mimics me, tutting in disappointment. "Oh, Clara, you should know that there's more to a country than the one region you've been to."

"Okay, you got me there," I say as we walk down a small hallway and board an elevator. "I've only been to the Great Wall of China and Beijing. What region is this food? Actually," I pause while we exit the elevator, "what's this restaurant called?"

"Fāyá," Nash says, pronouncing it Fah-yah. "And it's Sichuan."

A Chinese woman in a completely black outfit greets Nash by name, takes our coats, handing them off to another staff member, and beckons us to follow her. The space we've stepped into is almost completely black, and the staff nearly blends in. The walls and floors are black marble, the tablecloths are black, and even the view outside the floor-to-ceiling windows on the left is black. I can see shadows outside, and as we are led into the room Nash leans toward me. "Outside the window is a patio with a bamboo garden."

"Have you been here before?"

"No, but I've seen pictures."

While *most* of the room is black, there are notable exceptions. The same Chinese symbol from downstairs is repeated on the wall, backlit in red. There are small pendant lights hanging above each table, and the chairs are black lacquered wood with red embellishments. Everything is spaced out, and every seat is occupied. The room has a low murmur of conversation and traditional Chinese music, with strings and flutes.

We're seated at a two-person table. Our escort leaves after taking our drink order and setting the black napkins on our laps. The forks and knives on the table are black, too, but the chopsticks are black metal with red insets.

"Why'd you pick this place?" I ask, folding my hands on the table in front of me.

"I got a tip from a friend who's a restaurant critic. This place is new and relatively unknown right now. But it's going to be big, and it's already getting buzz."

"Look at you, ahead of the curve. And, excuse me," I hold up my hand like a school kid, "when did you become friends with a food critic?"

Nash smiles. "I do have friends outside of work."

I hold my silence, and after a few moments, Nash relents. "She's the girlfriend of one of my team members."

"Ah, so work-adjacent."

"Yes, well, it's brought us here, and I think you're going to love this place."

Nash glances over my shoulder and rises, stepping out from his chair. I look back, and a young Chinese-American man is approaching. It's slow going—he's escorting a tiny old lady through the room toward us.

"Mr. Deng," Nash says when they reach us.

"Mr. Darwish," the young man returns. He looks to be about our age, taller and leaner than Nash. He's sharply dressed, while the woman on his arm wears chef's garb—black pants, a white, pristine chef's jacket, and a matching skull cap.

Both men duck in a short bow, and Nash introduces me to the restaurateur.

"Please, call me Joe." He turns toward the old woman on his arm. "This is my grandmother, Fala Deng. She runs our kitchen," Joe says to us with an exaggerated wink.

Fala waves her hand and says something.

"Grandma says to please sit. She doesn't speak English, so I will translate for her." Joe himself has a New York accent but speaks to his grandmother in Mandarin. "She likes being out here, and she's prone to causing mayhem in the kitchen."

Nash and I take our seats, and Joe continues. "Our menu is prix fixe, focusing on one ingredient and incorporating it throughout the meal. Most of these dishes are ones my grandmother grew up making in her home in Sichuan. She cooked for four generations in one household."

Fala says more, still gesturing with her free hand. Joe tells us an abbreviated story of Fala's life, including leaving China and settling in New York. My admiration for the little old lady on his arm grows.

"The ingredient of the day is ginger," Joe says, bringing our attention back to the table. "It's used a lot in our cooking because it keeps so well and, especially on cold nights, it's revitalizing. Western medicine has only recently caught up to Eastern medicine in understanding the benefits of ginger. It's holistic; good for, as we would say here in America, the body and soul."

A server appears at my elbow and places a small plate in front of me. A matching plate is set in front of Nash at the same time.

"Duck confit with ginger and red date glaze," Joe says, and then he and his grandmother bow and wish us a good meal.

The duck skin is crisp and piping hot, the dark, moist meat arranged on top, the glaze, a thick brown like caramel, is used sparingly, and when I nimbly use the chopsticks to pop the whole amuse-bouche into my mouth, the skin snaps with a satisfying crackle.

"Oh my god," I say around my bite, but it comes out more like "eh ma gaww."

Nash can't even speak. He's just got his eyes closed while he chews.

"I don't even want to swallow it," I say.

We both sit in silence while we enjoy it. I gaze longingly at the drizzle of sauce on the plate.

"I'm sorry, did you say something? I think I blacked out," Nash says.

"This is too nice of a place to lick the plate, isn't it?"

"I have a reputation to maintain, Clara," Nash teases.

Joe appears at my elbow. "How was it?"

"It was the best thing I ever put in my mouth," I tell him, and then I play back those words in my head. Nash snorts, *loudly*, and covers his face with his napkin. "I mean, other than . . . obviously . . . "

When I gesture to Nash, he squeezes his eyes tight, shoulders shaking.

"I mean . . . "

Joe gazes up at the ceiling. When he finally looks back at me, the corner of his mouth trembles. "I'm glad you enjoyed it. I'll check back on you later."

As soon as Joe is out of earshot, Nash wheezes. "That's what she said." The last word comes out so high and squeaky I can barely hear it.

I put my face in my hands. "I can't believe I said that out loud."

Nash puts his face in his napkin again, and he's trying so hard to control himself that his eyes are welling.

"To be fair," I whisper across the table at Nash. "In all my years of saying that, I've never been at the table with someone who I've actually put in my mouth."

"Obviously, I don't take you out to good enough meals."

"How about this? That was the best thing I've ever put in my mouth under six inches."

Nash finally pulls the napkin down, and his smile is huge and contagious. As it fades, it shifts into something that makes my heart flutter—charmed. "I'll take the compliment."

"Anyway," I say, "I think that first course was worth the visit alone. Duck's always been my favorite."

"They certainly started out strong."

Nash and I smile at each other. This evening may be the most different thing we've ever done together. When I've seen Nash in the past, it's been family gatherings or lazy weekends in my dorm room or galas where Nash has work obligations. This feels more like a date. But here we are laughing our asses off and sharing jokes. I shouldn't have doubted that this would be any different.

"I was wondering." I rest my arms on the table and lean

forward. "Why did you pick tango lessons today? And the ballet? I'm a little surprised we didn't just spend the entire day pigging out."

Nash mirrors my pose. "I hope this doesn't come across as selfish, but I wanted to do some things for you and some things for me."

"I would never, ever think you are selfish, Nash." I hold his gaze, so he knows how much I mean it. "But dancing? For you? I had no idea you were interested in it."

"I used to watch *Dancing with the Stars*, which, of course, my parents would never allow, so I watched behind their backs. And then last year, Heartly had spare tickets to the New York City Ballet, and I'd never been. I saw *The Nutcracker* and was blown away. The grace of and strength of the dancers is inspiring, and seeing a performance like that was so outside of my wheelhouse. Although Ioann, the dancer in Central Park, is slightly better. He has more flare. Anyway, I've never been graceful or athletic. I certainly didn't grow up attending any kind of arts program."

Nash's gaze has wandered over my shoulder and into the distance as he's talked, and now he brings it back to focus on me. "I understand now that being well-rounded or not is a choice. And I don't have to choose to not be anymore," he says, relaxing back into his chair. "I've got season tickets now."

"That's amazing," I say. "You're lucky to live in a city that has such a great arts scene. And to be able to find something you enjoy as a hobby is really important." Nash's investment in the company and the city grows stronger every time I visit. Every new thing I hear about is noble—but also tethering.

Nash grins. "I might have been helped along by Uncle D. Seeing him trying to find hobbies in his partial retirement has been very entertaining."

"For the record, I think you are a fantastic dancer."

Nash's grin turns dirty. "You definitely demonstrated your appreciation."

I blush. The next course is set down in front of us—a Sichuanese variant of hot and sour soup. I lean forward and inhale the aroma, closing my eyes.

"Let me ask you something." I pick up the soup spoon that was delivered with our bowls. "You seem to know places I want to visit, places I've never been. What about you? Where do you want to go?"

I think about my answer. I know she wants something concrete, but the truth is I'd go anywhere, as long as it was with her, but that feels like cheating. I think it over while we sip our soup. The ginger and chili peppers warm me from the inside out, a pleasant feeling in winter.

"Is it that hard to think of one place you'd like to go?" Clara asks, concern knitting her eyebrows together.

"It's just hard to pick one place," I say, but I don't think she believes me. "How do you pick?"

"I don't have any difficulty picking where to go next. I want to go everywhere. I can't make the wrong decision."

"Everywhere is worth going, right?"

"Exactly. I'm not saying that I spin the globe and pick a location with my finger, but I read blogs and watch videos and do research." Clara's gesturing with her hands, the soup cooling in front of her while mine is almost gone. "Sure, I'm picking things based on the region I'm already in and what food opportunities there are, but people eat delicious food everywhere. Sydney is so full of interesting restaurants and chefs who are classically trained, but then I read about Javanese food and a Michelin-starred street hawker stall and

Malay dishes I'd never heard of before, and something just *pulls* me, you know?"

I don't, and Clara sees it in my face and frowns.

"When was the last time you went out of the country for fun?"

"We had that thing in Tokyo we went to."

She tilts her head. "That was a work conference for you, and I was already in Japan."

"But I had fun."

There's a pregnant pause, and Clara waits expectantly.

"All right," I admit. "I've never traveled for fun."

I expect Clara to say something encouraging, or suggest a trip together, but instead she smiles at me and shrugs casually. "It's a lifestyle not for everyone. I get that. But you've obviously shown me what amazing opportunities New York has." She gestures to the table. "This has been a very flavorful day."

She winks, and our empty soup bowls are swept up, and the next dish introduced: pig knuckles with pickled ginger and half a hardboiled egg.

It's not until we're drinking after-dinner tea—our sixth course, ginger and rice tea—when Clara shifts our conversation back to the day we've had.

"Is there another activity on the agenda? Dessert? Evening stroll? Flash mob dancing?"

I pull out my phone, texting our driver. "There is one thing on the menu," I tell her. "You."

"Finally," she teases.

"What do you mean, finally?" I lean in close to her. "You're not the one who's been sitting here thinking about how you said I was the second-best thing you've ever put in your mouth or about how I made you come on my hand just hours ago."

Clara visibly shivers, her eyes fluttering. They pop open, and she glances around. "Check, please!"

I laugh and put my napkin on the table. "It's taken care of. Let's go." I offer her my hand, and we twine our fingers together as I lead her back to the elevator and out to the car.

Clara sits close to me as the car pulls away from the curb, and my gaze falls to the dress she's wearing. With each pass of a streetlight, she sparkles. I part the lapels of her coat, the faux fur soft on my skin. She hums while my finger traces the geometric lace that starts at her left collarbone and swoops between her breasts and ends at her right hip.

"Kara did well, didn't she?" Clara murmurs.

"She's the best," I say. Unlike earlier in the changing room, Clara's languid, her eyes half closed as I press my lips against her neck. I can't decide which Clara I like more; the needy and urgent one who wants me so desperately or the one who's soft and simmering. Thank god I never have to choose.

She shifts, lifting her legs to my lap and her coat falls open further. I nip at her skin, making her gasp, and slide a hand to cup her breast.

The anticipation is the best part, and when I think about what I want to do to her—all the fantastic things we've done together in the past and things we've never done together before—I realize that tonight, despite all the planning that went into the entire day and yes, even the planning that went into tonight, I want to make love to Clara. Not just have sex but show her how I feel.

Her nipple is stiff under the silk, pebbling as I pinch it. "Nash," she whispers, and I find her mouth, open and panting, and kiss her bottom lip, that plump and soft pillow. Clara tries to kiss me back, but I pull away. "Nash," she says again, but this time on a whine.

The car rolls to a stop, and I glance up. We're outside my apartment, and I smile down at her. "We're here. Come on, baby."

I thank the driver and help Clara out of the car. The cold

nips at us during the few steps into the building, where I wave at the doorman and the elevator waits for us.

Clara wraps her hands around my waist and tugs me down to meet her as the doors close. Our kisses are slow and deliciously sensual.

Once we're inside my bedroom, I take two steps away from Clara and switch the bedside light on. "That's a nice dress; let me take it off you."

"In case I wear it again?" She laughs like it's a joke, but I hope someday that she will. Clara spins slowly so her back is to me. The zipper isn't hidden, the silver metal flashing in the soft lights of my room. Her hair is still up in the bun, so I kiss the back of her neck and lazily slide the tab down, my lips chasing my fingers.

By the time her underwear is revealed, a tiny black G-string, I'm on my knees. I've kissed every vertebra down to the thin fabric, and Clara shivers as the dress falls. "Stay right there," I whisper into her skin, and rise to my feet. Clara's facing the big window, so I strip quickly behind her and reach for the nightstand. I do have an ace in my back pocket that I've been looking forward to using all night.

When the drawer slides open, Clara calls out, "Nash?"

I pause, looking back at her. The soft glow of the light on her back is really fucking sexy.

She glances back at me. "I haven't . . . you know I haven't been with anyone since I was last with you, right?"

It takes me a moment to get what she's saying. "I'm not getting condoms," I clarify.

"Oh," she says, relieved.

"I told you I wasn't seeing anyone. Did you not believe me?"

"You said you hadn't been seeing anyone, but that doesn't mean you hadn't had sex," she explains. "I mean, a guy like you, it still boggles my mind."

I look back into the drawer and pick something from my

new collection. "Last time we were together, you told me you didn't own any toys."

"Yeah," she says, and now she's breathless and then laughing. "I always worry that my luggage will be searched or it'll turn on mid-flight and cause, like, a bomb scare or something."

I step up behind Clara and let my palm slide over her hip and to her stomach, pressing her back against me as we sit on the edge of my bed. "Well, I bought some."

Clara gasps when she sees the wand. While I bought a variety of toys, this is, to my understanding, the most powerful and reliable one. I've watched videos with couples using it and enjoyed it myself.

I maneuver Clara until her calves are on either side of mine, her legs spread open. My cock is hard and throbbing against her back, and she squirms. "I need you," she says as I press the head of the wand to the outside of her panties.

"Not yet," I say. This thing is powerful, and if I'm inside her while we're using it, I know I won't last long at all. "Ready?"

She just groans and grips my arms, bracing herself. I press the button, and she jolts.

"Holy shit."

"Too much?"

"No. No, no." One hand comes over mine, guiding the toy exactly where she wants it, and when she hits that spot, she bucks, pressing down on me.

"Oh, Jesus," she says, and the next few minutes are spent with Clara gasping and writhing on my lap. I use my other hand to band across her chest, pinning her down against mine. We're both sweaty and tense and panting.

Then she tightens, one hand gripping my knee hard, and I feel her body pulse, an orgasm wracking her.

"Okay, okay, okay, that's too much."

I chuckle and shift the wand away, pressing the button to turn it off. "Did you like it?" I whisper in her ear, nipping.

Clara's gone fully limp against me, and when she just hums, I laugh, my chest bouncing her up and down.

"Nash," she whines. "Please."

I turn, laying her on the bed and kissing my way down her body. Her legs fall open, and I carefully tug the G-string away from her damp pussy and down, throwing it to the floor. I give her a solid lick on my way back up, and she jerks beneath me, eyes flying open. We both laugh as I settle between her legs. She hitches one foot up, and I slide in.

I am proud of Clara's blissed-out face, and I nuzzle against the skin of her neck, pressing our palms together and threading my fingers with hers. I rock into her, gently pumping my hips. Everything about this is slower, lazy, loving. Clara gasps and moans, but it's nothing like the rushed heat from this afternoon or the explosiveness from her last orgasm.

Instead, this one is quiet, intimate. I come watching her eyes fall closed, her lips parted on a shuddering, satisfied breath.

11

NASH

THE MORNING IS SLOW AND LAZY AGAIN. CLARA WAKES ME WITH whispered words in my ear, words that are intended to spur me on but only make my heart clench.

"I want you again before I go," she says.

She straddles my hips and sinks onto me, her chest hovering over mine. We rock together, her hair a curtain over the left side of my face, her morning breath against my cheek. I'm not nineteen anymore, so a third round in twelve hours might be impossible, but that's how it is with Clara, feast or famine.

She shifts to press herself just how she needs it against me, and I let my fingers dig into her hips. Her forehead leaves mine and drops to the pillow as she shudders through her climax. I stroke her back while she catches her breath, and then she starts again.

I feel my orgasm dragging up from the depths, slowly building from my toes while she rocks against me. Clara gets antsy on top of me, her legs stretch out along mine, and she grinds harder. I clench my ass, thrusting up to help her.

"I'm getting close again," she says before biting my shoulder.

"Harder," I say. I want a mark I'll see for the next few days, something that'll catch my eye in the mirror and remind me that I had her here.

Clara's teeth dig in, and I wince until she lets go, the blood rushing back to the spot where her teeth were. She shifts again. "Nash." It's a warning.

My hands glide down her back and cup her butt, grabbing and squeezing. "Clara, I'm coming."

Her muscles under my hand flex and then we're both pulsing, hips twisting and trying to stretch it out as long as we can. Clara bites me again, gentler this time, and moans against my skin.

In the aftermath, Clara draws her legs up, pressing her knees against my sides. I soften inside of her until we make a mess on my abs and Clara sighs dramatically.

"All right, I guess I need to get up and get going."

There's so much resignation in her voice, it gets my hopes up. "You could stay, you know. As long as you want."

Clara pulls herself upright, carefully swinging her leg to dismount, and uses a tissue to wipe between her legs. "I can't. Flight's at four."

Before I can answer, she walks into the bathroom, closing the door behind her.

I grab my own tissue and clean up. We take turns showering and then dress. I get distracted watching Clara shimmy into her yoga pants and sports bra. She throws a light-weight, long-sleeve shirt over it, her usual airplane outfit, which makes my heart clench.

Soon, we're out in the kitchen, and I start cooking breakfast. Clara sits on the counter—completely in the way—while I cook.

We joke and laugh until a buzz sounds from my doorbell. Clara and I glance at each other.

"Who could that be?" she asks.

I stride over to the intercom, pressing the button. "Yes?"

"Mr. Darwish, Fritz Cohen is here to see you."

I throw a glance over my shoulder at Clara.

What is my brother doing here? She mouths.

"You know he can't hear you, right?"

She rolls her eyes. "Nash! Seriously, what is he doing here?"

"I have no idea. He's never been here before." I press the button again. "Let him up," I say to the doorman.

Clara crosses her arms over her chest. "My dads know, and now Fritz is going to find out."

"Is that such a bad thing?"

Clara's eyes go soft at my tone. "It's not, but I liked having you all to myself."

"It's been nearly a decade, Clara." I take a deep breath, reining in my patience. A knock comes from the door. "You ready?" I ask.

"As ever," she responds, and her resignation makes me grind my jaw.

I open the door, and Fritz hits me with a punch in the face.

12

CLARA

"Nash!" I scream. He falls back, landing on the ground with a hard oomph.

"Motherfu—" Fritz starts, shaking his hand and curling his body around it, his face etched in pain.

"Fritz, what the fuck is wrong with you?" I land on my knees next to Nash as he rises up on an elbow. His other hand is cupping his face, and blood is dripping from between his fingers.

Instead of answering me, Fritz sucks in air through his teeth as if *his* pain is unbearable.

I pull Nash's hands away from his face. Fritz punched him on his left jaw, and the area is red and swelling quickly, the lip on that side cut. I help Nash stand. "Come on, let's get ice on that."

"Don't you see, Clara," my brother says. "He's just using you."

We ignore him, walking to Nash's kitchen. "You're an idiot," I tell my brother over my shoulder. In the kitchen, I grab a cold can of soda and give it to Nash to hold against his face while I dig out a plastic bag and fill it with ice.

Instead of leaving—*read the room, Fritz*—he follows us into the kitchen and has the *gall* to ask for ice for his hand. I glare at him for a moment and give the ice to Nash.

Nash hands the ice over to Fritz, who sniffs and takes it. I put my hands on my hips and swivel my glare to Nash. "Why?"

"I've got this." Nash raises the soda back to his jaw as if the ice is what I'm talking about.

"No. Why? Why are men so stupid?" I return my glare to my brother. "Why, exactly, did you think it was a good idea to punch Nash? Never mind the fact that he could—and *should*—sue your ass."

Fritz glares at Nash. "He's using you to get Uncle D's company."

"That makes no sense," I snap.

"He's seducing you! He wants your share of the company."

I clench my jaw. "Once again, Fritz, that makes no sense."

"He told Dad he's going to marry you. Obviously, that's his plan to gain control of the company."

Oh, for fuck's sake . . .

"Companies don't work that way," I tell Fritz. "Maybe a few years ago, that would have worked, but the company is publicly traded now."

Uncertainty flickers in Fritz's expression. "I know that. But still—"

"And, even if the company wasn't publicly traded, Uncle D has an exit strategy that's being implemented over the next few years. Who I marry has absolutely nothing to do with Heartly."

"But you'd still be rich," Fritz insists.

"And so would Nash," I shout. "We all three inherit from Uncle D and Dad if anything were to happen."

"We do?" Nash and Fritz say at the same time.

"Yes, we do. Nash is practically family regardless of whether I was to marry him or not."

The two of them stare at me. "How do you know this?" Nash asks.

"Because Uncle D and I talk about these kinds of things. He's always been a business mentor to me. Maybe not as much as he's been to you, but ever since my first pitch to him, he talks to me about things, too, including the new wills Uncle D and Dad had written a few years ago."

"You pitched to Uncle D? Why did you need to pitch to him?" Fritz's forehead is scrunched up, and by god, this proves that my brother has no idea what goes on in the business.

"Uncle D gave me the seed money for my first year of travel. I put together a five-year strategic plan, and he lent me the money."

Fritz's jaw drops. "He refused to loan me money when I wanted to invest in Duke's farm."

"Duke's farm was for fish oil pills, and he didn't have a five-year business plan or FDA approval. He lasted six months, and god knows what happened to the idiots who invested in him."

"*I* invested in him." Fritz clenches his jaw, and the room goes quiet. I'm not going to say it out loud, but I'm still thinking it—god, my brother is an idiot.

"You never were that interested in Heartly, anyway," I say, turning us back to the point at hand. "If you'd put any effort in, then maybe you'd actually have something to argue about."

"So what? That's it? You're going to marry Nash?"

"No, I'm not," I sputter.

Fritz looks between the two of us, and Nash is, oddly, silent.

"Where did you even hear that?" I ask Fritz.

"There's a picture of you all over social media kissing in the subway station. I went over to Dad's place to see what it was all about, and Dad said Nash wanted to marry you."

"That's not what's happening here," I tell my brother.

Fritz narrows his eyes at Nash. "Unless you just said that to make our dads feel better."

"I didn't say it to make them feel better," Nash says.

We're quiet again while I stare at Nash. Did he just say . . . did he just insinuate that he wants to *marry me*?

That draws me up short. When? Why? Nash and I have always just kept our relationship casual . . . haven't we?

I shake the thoughts out of my head, returning to the main problem.

Nash stands from the stool and approaches my brother. "Hey Fritz, I think it's time to go."

My brother eyes me warily.

"Go," I tell him. "This isn't about you."

He huffs and spins around, walking away from this bomb he's detonated in the middle of my quiet morning with Nash. The front door slams, and Nash turns to me. There's a look on his face I've never seen before; wary and hopeful and appre-hensive.

He hasn't denied it, but I don't understand what's happening. We've been friends for so long, sleeping together for so long. If Nash had feelings for me, how come he didn't say anything? How could it have gone on for this long without one of us breaking?

The only thing that makes sense to me is that Nash didn't say it.

"What, exactly, did you say to my dad?"

"I told your dad that I was going to marry you." He holds my gaze steady, a juxtaposition to my heart fluttering in my chest.

"Let me get this straight. You didn't say you wanted to marry me or ask for his permission to propose. You didn't even talk to me about it. You just said you were going to marry me?"

"Yes."

"Nash," I say, bringing my hands to my temples and rubbing. "What does that even mean? I don't understand what that would look like. And why would you even say something like that without having given *any* thoughts to my opinion?"

This is not like Nash at all. Where's the guy that talks to me about everything? Where's the man who supports me while I get to make my own decisions about my life?

"I know that this wasn't ideal," he says, and the placation in his tone irks me, "but here's the truth: I'm in love with you. I've been in love with you for a very long time. And I know you're in love with me, too, and you're panicking right now."

"I'm not panicking," I snap. "You think you know me so well, but you don't. We see each other, what? Maybe twice a year if we're lucky?"

"Clara, I've known you for decades. I know the places you've been and the places you want to go. I know that you are so good at what you do because you are so positive, and you work harder than anyone I know, even myself." Nash reaches out, grabbing my hand and using it to tug me closer. "I know the way you feel pressed up against me." He turns my hand over, bringing the sensitive skin of my wrist to his mouth, and kisses the hammering pulse underneath. I'm frozen in place, rooted to the floor. "I know the noises you make when I kiss you just the way you like it and how your breath catches when you come." He nuzzles into my hand, and the skin under my palm is soft and smooth. "I know your skin is so delicate, you like me to shave. Believe me, Kara's been trying to get me to grow some stubble out, but I'd never do it because you like it like this."

"Nash—"

"I know you so well, Clara. I know you're never going to be finished because you'll never feel like you've done enough to satisfy this wanderlust within you. You're chasing this idea to experience things that your mom never got to experience.

But she also had her family and loved hard. I would love you with everything I have."

"This isn't just about love." I pull my hand back, extricating it from his grip, upset all over again that my hand is shaking. "This is about how I live wherever I want. Your whole life is here in New York, and my whole life is doing everything I can to make my business work. It's a hustle, and it's hard as hell. You *know* this." My voice is desperate. I wish we could go back in time and start all over. I wouldn't try to creep into bed with Nash, I wouldn't pretend that he was my boyfriend all day, I wouldn't kiss him in public because neither of us needs this drama.

"You can change your plans. This is your business, and you should run it however you want, and if you really want this relationship, we could make it work."

"So you want me to drop everything I'm doing, my business plans, my strategies, the connections I've made, so that I can stay with you?" My voice is raised now, nearly shouting. "Do you *know* how many bridges I would burn? I have people depending on me. I may not be responsible for the whole of Heartly, but I have small businesses who are planning for my help with their promotions. I have plans that, if canceled, would have wasted so many people's time and money."

"I'm not asking you to cancel your plans. I'm just saying that you could compromise a little bit."

"What does that look like? What does my compromise look like? What does your compromise look like?"

"Think about everything we did here in the city yesterday. It wasn't just a preview. These people, these cultures, are real and here. You could do something with that."

"That's what yesterday was about? It wasn't about us spending time together or having fun; it was manipulation. It was you telling me to change my business. It was you having an agenda for our lives that you wouldn't even talk to me about."

"No, it wasn't—"

I barrel right over him. "And let's talk about compromise, Nash. All I've ever wanted in life is to travel, and I'm not going to stop doing that. But what about you? You want to compromise, but what are you compromising for me? You work so much that you never take vacation. You've got a million things tying you down to this city, and that's not how I'll live my life."

"We can sit down and figure this out together."

"When Nash?" I pressed a hand to my chest, feeling my heart racing along. I thought we'd go out quietly, not like this. Not with a crash and burn. "My flight is today, and you're springing this whole idea on me that we should be together."

"Clara." There's something in his voice this time that sharpens my focus. "This isn't out of nowhere. You have to know how I feel on some level."

"I'm not a mind-reader," I retort.

"All right," he says, irritatingly calm. "Then you must know how you feel about me."

The silence hangs between us, and I search myself for any kind of answer that wouldn't completely upend my life, and there isn't one. "I have to go," I say. "I have lunch with my parents."

"Clara . . ."

I spin around and dart down the hall, gathering my purse. Kara had left me an overnight bag here, and I stuff all of my things into it.

Except for my dress. This stunning gem of a dress that I will probably never wear again doesn't deserve to be crammed into my bag. Instead, I throw open the door to Nash's closet to dig out a hanger. When the light snaps on, I freeze.

The closet is huge, with rows of neatly organized suits on

one side, a shoe rack full of leather that shines, big, square cubbies that hold folded soft sweaters, and drawers that hide away the rest.

But the left side of the closet is mostly empty. There were a few dozen hangers, multicolored fabrics trembling from the force of the wind when I opened the door.

I run a hand over the first item that stands out. It's a dress I wore to a gala, the one in the magazine article, bright blue with a nearly-indecent slit. Next to it is a summer dress I wore two years ago when Nash took me to a museum. Then there are three dresses I recognize from yesterday, the ones that Kara had as backups for last night.

The rest is a simple collection of pajamas, shirts, sweaters, and jackets, classic staples that are all in my size. Whatever I would need to be comfortable for a few days, no matter the weather or the time of year.

It's pathetic how this makes me feel. I'm sure Kara bought these things, but I'm also certain that Nash is the one who asked her to do it, who paid for it, who leaves half of his closet open, waiting for me to take up space in his life.

Numb, I pick an empty hanger and fasten the pink dress on. The silver strands catch the light and blur while my eyes fill.

Does Nash live like this in every aspect of his life? Just waiting for me to take my place? My heart breaks for Nash, and I wish that he'd said something or that we'd been smarter about how we treated each other. If I'd known . . .

Would things be any different? Would our relationship have ended years ago?

I don't bother checking the bathroom for any of my things. I just sling the bag over my shoulder and exit the room. Nash is still in the kitchen.

"Clara—" he starts, rising to his feet.

I cut him off. I don't want to hear how Nash thinks I should change my life. I don't want to think about how lonely he is and what expectations he had for us. I feel deceived and like this whole thing has blown up in my face, and this isn't how I wanted my few days off to end. "I'll see you next time, Nash. Okay?"

And I leave without waiting for a response.

13

NASH

I lay low for a few days, licking my wounds. The office is closed anyway, so I work from home, throwing myself into planning a coding event in January for one of our outreach programs for disadvantaged neighborhoods.

It's the day before New Year's Eve, though, and I'm supposed to be going to a big party with Craig and Uncle D. I've been thinking about canceling, giving my ticket to someone else. I'm in no mood to celebrate anything.

How could I have let things get so out of hand? My day with Clara was supposed to be fun and an adventure, not destroying our relationship.

Believe me, I've tried to talk myself out of loving Clara so often, but what I always circle back to is the way that she makes me feel.

And I've just made her feel like shit.

This was not how any of this was supposed to go.

I realized I was in love with Clara on a random Spring Tuesday. I hadn't seen her in months, not since she came to New York in January for three days on a long layover, and we babysat the then-eight-month-old twins. I have no idea what possessed us to care for two crawling babies, but it had been hilarious and exhausting.

A few months later, Clara had messaged me a random picture of her with a baby on her lap while she was somewhere in Brazil and the message *Aren't they so much better when you can give them back?*

I had looked at the photo and saw her with a baby that could have been ours—darker skin, a shock of black hair, and a toothy grin—and realized that my missing her was more than just as a best friend, more than just someone I slept with.

I wanted everything with Clara.

And now I've fucked it up.

See? My mood is sulky and morose with a dash of spiraling. I'm not fit for company.

Which is why I ignore the buzzer at my door. I wouldn't have even heard it except that I was grabbing a cold beer in the kitchen before going back to my office.

But the buzzing is insistent, which means they've probably been buzzing for a while. If I don't answer soon, they are likely to get in trouble with the doorman.

"Hello?" I say, pressing the button.

"Naaaassshhhhhh!" A tiny child's wail comes through the speaker.

"Molly?" I ask, completely confused.

"And us," Whitney says in the background. "Molly didn't think you were going to answer and is having a meltdown."

I shift on my feet. I can't say no, either to Molly or Whitney. I push the button again. "Is Fritz with you?"

"Yes." That voice belongs to him, and Molly's wailing is slowly dying down. "Can we please come up?"

"Only if you promise not to punch me."

There's a beat of silence, and then I hear an oof, like someone's elbow had an impact with someone else's ribs.

"I promise not to punch you . . . as long as you don't say anything stupid."

"Seriously?" I hear Whitney reprimand her husband. "You can't even be pleasant through the intercom?"

"He's sleeping with Clara!"

"Cut it out with the patriarchal bullshit."

Whitney's voice is rising, and now I'm worried they're going to get in trouble with security for an entirely different reason.

"I'm buzzing you up."

I wait at my door, listening for the ding of the elevator. Molly leads the charge coming out, barreling toward my apartment, her brother holding Whitney's hand and moving at a much more sedate pace.

"Uncle Nash!" Molly screams and barrels into my legs. I swiftly pick her up under the armpits, which makes her squeal, and I move us inside before my neighbors complain. "I learned a new word today," she tells me, poking my three-day-old scruff.

"Yeah? What word did you learn?" I ask as I lead Fritz's family inside. Ricky is struggling with his jacket, so he and Fritz stay by the door and wrestle with it while I lead Whitney in. Benny is strapped to her chest, and she has a diaper bag hanging off one shoulder. With a thunk, it lands on my kitchen counter, and Whitney starts rooting around in the side pockets.

"Patry-cal." She says it with a kick of her little feet, except one of them lands directly on my crotch and lightning shoots up from my balls. My knees clench together, and I sink down to kneeling, trying not to topple Molly onto the marble floor. "And bullshit!" she shouts in my ear.

Now I'm throbbing at both ends.

"Sure, that's the word she can pronounce correctly," Whitney mutters as she unstraps Benny.

Molly giggles as I clench my eyes shut.

"What are you doing?" Fritz's voice hovers over me, and

when I crack my eyes open, he's looking down at me, befuddled.

"Got kicked in the nuts," I tell him with a gasp.

"Ah, yeah. She's gotten really kicky lately. Nails me twice a week." He frowns. "Molly, why don't you give Uncle Nash a break, and let's play I Spy out his window?"

Molly dismounts me, shouting, "I spy something red!" before running to the window. From where I'm sitting, I can only see blue sky and clouds, so who knows what the hell she sees.

Fritz looks at Ricky. "Go play with your sister."

Ricky meanders to the window, despite Molly's shouts for him to hurry up, finger digging in his nose the whole time.

Fritz returns his gaze to me and offers me a hand. I accept it.

"You get used to it after a while," he says while hauling me upright.

"Says the man who instigated the first incidence of violence on me this week," I grind out. I stagger a few steps away to the couch.

"Yeah," he says, running a hand over his hair and taking the seat across from me. "I wanted to apologize about that."

"How much of this apology is you, and how much of it is Whitney making you?"

He considered the question. "About seventy-thirty."

Figures. Whitney's always the one that whips Fritz into shape.

Fritz leans a little closer. "The seventy is me, by the way. I am sorry about punching you."

"I'm not sorry I slept with your sister."

Fritz blanches. "Gross."

"It's not gross!" Whitney shouts from the kitchen. "She's a grown, consenting adult!"

I give Fritz a small smile. "Forgiven."

"Whitney's here mostly because she wants to meddle," he says.

"I heard that." Whitney appears from behind me, lifting the carrier up and over my head as she passes between the couch and armchair. She fusses with Benny for a moment, setting the carrier on the floor at her feet and tucking him in, and then she sits, keeping an eye on her baby.

Fritz waves a hand dramatically at me. "Commence meddling."

Whitney's eyes light up, and she lightly claps her hands together. "Tell us everything that went down between you and Clara."

I groan. "Come on, I don't want to relive that."

"You have to. How else are you going to get a plan together? You had your big chance, and it got blown—" she looks pointedly at her husband, "—so it's time to call in the reinforcements. Tell us how you fucked up, and we'll try to fix it."

By keeping our relationship secret, Clara and I have never had to deal with this kind of meddling. It means we've never been pressured to talk to anyone else. Although, now that I think about it, I remember when Bea, and then Kara, found out and the relief of talking to them.

And I wonder if Clara has told anyone in her life about me. Would she have talked about me to her newest friends that she's made in Australia? Or caught her online friends up on what a moron I've been?

So I tell them everything. I tell them about how I've loved Clara for years and how I wanted her to see that New York would be a place she could love.

"That is pretty manipulative," Fritz says.

Great. Now Fritz is smarter than me.

"It's not like I could just say, 'hey, maybe you should scale back your work and hang out with me more often.' That's less manipulative but still a bonehead move."

"Bonehead!" Molly shouts from the dining room where she and Ricky are coloring.

"Well, you suggested she change a lot," Whitney points out, "but what are you changing?"

"I guess . . . nothing. I thought Clara would be ready to move back here someday, and clearly, she's not. It makes sense to me because my whole life is here, and Clara's family is here, but the rest of her life is anywhere but here. Clara pointed out that I've never even taken a trip somewhere fun."

"'Be the change you want to see in the world,'" Fritz says.

Whitney and I stare at him. "Did you just quote Gandhi?" I ask.

"I don't think it was Gandhi," he says. "But whoever it was, I think they just told you to take a vacation."

14

CLARA

I call Dad from the ship in Sydney Harbour where I watched the fireworks show half an hour ago. "Hello from the future!" I say when he answers.

"Hey, Sugar Plum, how's life in the new year?"

I make a big show of looking around, even though Dad can't see me. "Looks about the same."

"Figures. Where are you right now?"

I tell him about the cruise I've been on, about the view of the Sydney Opera House and the Sydney Harbour Bridge and the fireworks show from the top of a forty-meter vessel.

"Sounds amazing. Oh, guess who's here," he says. I suck in my breath. I wondered if Nash was spending the evening with them, but I haven't spoken to him or asked about him since I left his apartment on December twenty-seventh.

I thought I would be mad for longer, but I had barely sat down on the first airplane before I replayed the whole thing from a different perspective.

The *what if* perspective.

What if one of us had said, that first weekend Nash visited me at college, that we wanted more than a casual thing? What if after college, I'd gotten a career in the travel industry instead of forging my own path?

What if I'd spent more time with Nash, even just a week. Would I have fallen in love with him? Did I ever even give Nash a chance?

By the time I arrived in Sydney, I realized that I was very good at compartmentalizing Nash, putting him in a New York City-shaped box, and keeping him at arm's length because I had somewhere else to be.

There's some clicking around and background noises, and then I hear Uncle D's voice. "Happy New Year."

I return the greeting, relaxing. Of course, he meant Uncle D. Why am I disappointed to talk to my favorite stepdad?

"Is your trip to Sydney everything you were hoping for?" Uncle D asks.

"So far, yeah. I did the opera house tour and climbed the bridge and a bunch of other fun things. No kangaroo or koala sightings yet, but I'm headed up the coast after this. How are things at home?"

"Good."

There's a pregnant pause, and I can picture Uncle D's steady gaze, waiting for me to break down and ask what I really want to know: How's Nash?

And then, through the phone, I hear a buzzing noise.

"Clara, I have to go," Uncle D says regretfully. "But real quick, we're going to be in Singapore next Tuesday. Where will you be?"

"Um . . ." I mentally flip through my schedule. "Ningaloo Reef, on the west coast of Australia."

"Send me details, maybe I can see you. Love you."

I laugh, but Uncle D is already gone. Sure, why not just a hop skip and a jump across three thousand kilometers to see me? Never mind the fact that I'll be on a boat.

Shaking my head, I message Uncle D with the details while I'm thinking about it. And then my thumb wanders of its own accord to Instagram. I check Nash's account—not his public one, but his private one, the one that was my very first follower all those years ago. He doesn't post his face, obviously, but usually, I can get a clue about what he's been up to lately.

Tonight, though, no dice. He hasn't posted anything since I last saw him. I scroll his feed, and it's like a montage of daily life in New York—new food, friends, and places. I don't recognize any of them.

I switch apps and look at my photos from our day together. I haven't posted anything yet, but flipping through them now, after my fight with Nash, I see things I didn't see before, like the street signs in Arabic by the spice market and the faces of the people around us at the Sri Lankan restaurant.

It's been four days. Not that long in the grand scheme of things. I'm barely over my jet lag from the flight here.

Going four days without talking isn't unusual for us. So why do I feel so lonely? Is it because I've just seen my family and had the warm and fuzzies over spending the holidays with everyone? Or is it something deeper . . . something that feels suspiciously like a Nash-shaped hole in my heart.

I shake my head and put my phone away. I'm on a yacht in Sydney Harbour. I'm *working*. I need to get out of this funk and move on. Nash is in New York; his life is in New York. And I am everywhere but there.

"Do you hear that?" Nancy, one of the other guests, asks a week later. She's seated next to me at the lunch table on the yacht *Galatea*. We're between dives and pretty much stuffing our faces with as much food as we can during our break. Doing three dives a day is exhausting, but it's peak turtle season in Ningaloo Reef, and we all want to see as much as possible. And, of course, that means absolutely pigging out on the locally caught seafood and wild game the chef is serving.

"Is that our boat?" someone else asks.

It's a faint hum, which could be the sound of the electric engines underneath us but doesn't feel quite right.

"Yeah, nah, it sounds like a plane," one of the Aussie guys down the table says. I've grown used to these cute Aussie-isms like "yeah, nah" and "nah, yeah," which might be, like drop bears, designed to confuse tourists. We all crane our necks, looking at the sky surrounding us.

"There it is," says Nina, one of the staff onboard.

We all point to where she's looking, and yeah, there's a low-flying plane. This part of Australia is remote—the state of Western Australia is pretty much desert, and the nearest town, Exmouth, is hours away. The airport, which was built more to serve the military base than the town, is even further away.

The plane grows closer and lower. Eric, the captain of the boat, leaves the table and climbs up the stairs to the pilot house. When the plane swoops close enough, the Aussie guy takes a sharp breath.

"Oh, damn. That's an Icon A5."

"What does that mean?" someone asks.

"It's a really bloody fancy seaplane."

Sure enough, I can see the floats at the base of the plane. We're all out on deck now, watching as the plane passes over-head and then does a wide bank to circle back. This time it drops lower and lower. . . .

"Holy shit, it's going to land," Nancy exclaims.

With a roar, the seaplane touches down, gracefully slowing a few hundred yards away from our boat.

And my heart starts to flutter. What if . . . ? No, he wouldn't. That would be crazy. There is no way Nash would travel all the way out here to see me.

"Dee, Jason." We all crane our necks up to see Captain Eric looking down at us. "We've got company," he tells the crew.

I stand with the rest of the guests and watch the seaplane aim toward the back of the boat. The closer it gets, the faster my heart beats. The noise of the prop dies, and the door to the plane opens. The pilot steps out onto the pontoons, walking nimbly as the plane slows to a perfect stop next to the boat. He throws a line to Dee, who catches it and ties off.

The seaplane pilot walks around to the passenger door and opens it. I hold my breath. A closely shaven head ducks down and climbs out of the seat.

My jaw drops. "Uncle D?"

"Hey, Sugar Plum." He gives me a wave while making his way down the float and toward the deck of *Galatea*. The pilot and our crew help him step aboard the boat, and there's a lot of murmuring behind me from the other guests.

My stomach sinks. It's not Nash. He's not coming here to find me in the middle of nowhere, Australia.

Oh shit.

I'm not just disappointed that it's not Nash—I'm heartbroken.

Captain Eric appears next to me and offers Uncle D a hand. "Pleasure to have you aboard, sir."

"Thank you. Lovely boat you have here." Uncle D greets him and then sticks his hands in his pockets. He's wearing board shorts. *Board shorts*. Where is my boardroom-dominating, three-piece-suit-wearing stepdad?

Uncle D leans in, looking into my eyes, which are welling up. He gives me a soft smile in understanding.

"Would you like a tour?" Eric asks.

"Thank you, but I'm short on time. Do you have a room where my daughter and I can talk?"

Eric gestures for us to follow him, and I grab the towel I was sitting on and fall in next to Uncle D.

"Don't you think that was a little extra?" I choke out at him.

"I'd never been in a seaplane before. That's one off the bucket list."

Uncle D has a bucket list?

Eric leads us to the steep ladder to the top deck and opens the door for us, telling us to take all the time we need. The pilot house is nice; black leather in the main pedestal chair at the center and two matching benches on either side of the room.

Uncle D opens his arms to me, and even though I'm damp and salty, I sink into his embrace. He waits, patting my head while I take big, deep breaths of the man who's been a rock-steady figure in my life.

Finally, I pull away. I'm not crying but it's close.

I settle my towel on the closest bench, and Uncle D sits next to me.

"Since when do you have a bucket list?" I ask him instead of diving into deeper stuff.

"I'm sure everyone has a mental bucket list," Uncle D muses. "But I took the time to write one down last week. Nash was doing one, and Craig and I thought it would be a good idea to make our own. And then he told me we had to do one of the trips right now, and what a coincidence, it took us near you."

I focus on Nash's name. "Nash? He made a bucket list?"

Uncle D nods. "He had a good point. Craig and I still haven't spent much time doing fun things, and as you know, I am *supposed* to have more free time since we're transitioning me out of the business. I have been focusing on hobbies, but I think getting us out on trips is a pretty great idea."

"But *Nash*. Nash has a bucket list?"

"Not only does he have a bucket list, but he took a month off work. It was a little bit troublesome at first, but I'm learning to work with his temporary replacement, Peter."

"Do you know what's on his bucket list?"

"I think you should ask him yourself, Sugar Plum."

I consider that Uncle D probably has a point, so I direct the conversation back to him. "What else is on your bucket list?"

He ticks a few things off his fingers, including Kyoto.

"You know I've been to Kyoto, right?"

"Where do you think I got the inspiration from?" he asks me with a smirk. I grin, but then the smile slips from his lips.

"So, Nash is out trying to expand his worldview." Uncle D rubs his cheek, the rasp of his hand on his stubble filling the silence. "What happened there, Sugar Plum?"

I sigh and stare out the window. There's nothing but blue all around us, with splotches of browns and tans marking the reef.

"I'm not the right person for Nash."

"Why?"

"Because he lives in New York. He's so happy doing what he does, and I need to be out here. This is my entire life, and I can't be stagnant."

"Is this a money issue? Cause you could pitch me for another investment."

"No, it's not about money. I'm basically covering all my operating costs now."

"So it's an emotional issue?"

"It's not."

A smile flirts across his lips. "The lady doth protest too much."

"That's not what's happening here," I say. It's supposed to come out as a joke, but it dies into sadness, and I feel tears welling up.

"Hey," Uncle D's tone sweetens, and he leans forward, taking my hand in his. "Do you love Nash?"

"Of course I do." The words are quick, like *of course I love him, he's practically family*, but Uncle D doesn't take my bull-shit and waits me out.

I dig for the truth, for honesty that most people would never pull out of me, but Uncle D is exactly that person to make me stop and think. I value his opinion on everything from my business to my family.

And I realize that these last few weeks have been grayscale for me. I'm less excited about everything that I'm doing. I'm missing my usual spunk and excitement. I told myself that if I didn't love Nash, he wouldn't break my heart someday. But here I am, brokenhearted anyway. And maybe even worse than I would be otherwise because Nash chose me, Nash loves me, and I was the one who was too scared to try to figure out how to make it work.

And for what? My business is successful. I've traveled more than I could have ever dreamed when I first started out. Maybe even more than my mom had ever dreamed of traveling.

Because when it came down to it, she chose family instead. While I found that sad at first . . . now that I'm years into this endeavor, I'm not so sure.

I answer more honestly, more seriously this time. "I do. But I always thought that he'd find someone more well-suited for him. I'm never there. I work my ass off on the road, and he works his off in New York. The timing's never been right for us, it's never going to be right for us."

"Maybe you weren't ready for him right out of college when you started looking at your blog as a business. Maybe you weren't ready for him a year ago. But why aren't you ready now?"

"I'm not ready to give up traveling."

"Did he ask you to?"

It takes a moment for me to think back. What was it exactly that Nash said? "He asked me to compromise."

"Can you compromise?"

"He had plenty of ideas for me to compromise. It was easy for him to see me staying in New York and giving things up. But how is he going to meet me halfway?"

"Can I give you some business advice?"

I blink at the change of topic, and Uncle D gives me a wry smile. "Umm . . . I guess?"

"A lot of what made us successful in business was pivoting. When we got an opportunity, as long as it aligned with our long-term goals and missions, we took it. Being nimble was a part of why we were able to take advantage of the code Nash wrote. Other companies might have said that it wasn't in the five-year plan or that it wasn't what the market was doing and it wasn't worth the time. But together, Nash and I and the rest of our team figured out how to pivot the business and make it work."

"So, I should . . . pivot?"

Uncle D shrugs. "You've had an opportunity come up. If there's something you want, you should figure out a way that you can have the thing that makes you happy—like time off with your partner or checking some items off your bucket list —while still keeping to the core of who you are and your goals. And actually," he stands up, straightening the buttons of his shirt, "you might find that one goal benefits the other. Is it worth asking Nash if he's willing to make changes?"

What would I ask Nash to do? Just because I can't see us working out with the changes he suggested doesn't mean we wouldn't work out other ways.

"Now, give me a kiss so I can pass it along to your dad when I see him today."

"Dad's here?" I ask with surprise.

"He's waiting in Exmouth. Could not convince him to get on that seaplane."

"Figures. Dad has always been a little nervous about planes. If he hasn't gotten used to it by now, I doubt he ever will."

Uncle D opens the door for me, and the sea breeze rushes in. "The time you flew in a glider is still the only video of yours he's never seen."

I roll my eyes and lead the way down the ladder. "Where are you and Dad going next?"

"Sydney. While I'm in the country, I've been asked to stop by the office there. And I promised your dad I would take him to the opera house for a show."

We find Uncle D's pilot hanging out with the ship's crew. The guests have spread out over the boat, napping or sunbathing until our lunch settles and we get to dive again.

"So," Uncle D says, turning to me. "Should I say anything to Nash?"

I gaze off into the distance and consider my answer. "No," I finally say. "I think I have a presentation to put together."

15

NASH

Why haven't I been doing this all along?

The neon blue water of the Caribbean laps at my feet. It's actually chilly, though with the sun beating down as strongly as it is today, I'm warm enough that the cold water feels good.

I'm sitting in a lounge chair, my feet in a few inches of crystal-clear water, and aside from the gentle swell of the sea, there's hardly any sounds. The resort I'm staying at is popular but spacious enough to give me alone time, which means that I've crossed three items off my bucket list today:

-Visit the Caribbean

-Enjoy some alone time

-Don't use technology for 24 hours

The last one is obviously the hardest, but the resort is having a technology-free weekend. The Wi-Fi is off, my laptop is back in New York, and my phone, without an international plan and Wi-Fi, is essentially a brick, so I readily handed it over at the front desk, which offers to "confiscate" technology to keep you honest for the weekend.

This first trip was surprisingly easy to plan. I picked a place Clara had been to, a place she'd written about. It was stupid of me because I spent too long studying the pictures of the resort. Most of them didn't have her in the shot, but a few did, and now I'm seeing these places in person and thinking of Clara.

There's the hammock in the over-water palapa that Clara lazed about in one afternoon.

This is the shrimp mofongo she raved about.

I wonder if this is the bungalow she stayed in.

I did it because there was no one I trusted more to plan my first fun vacation than Clara.

I've been thinking about her a lot. The suggestions Whitney, Fritz, and I came up with are pretty good, but the idea of talking to Clara without testing my ideas out felt hollow.

So here I am, on a real-world user-experience test. It's a chance to prove to myself that I can do the kinds of things Clara would need me to do. I can travel with her, occupy myself while she works, and spend time away from my job.

And explore. Now I'm in the Caribbean. Next is a week in Italy, and after that, Cape Town. A whole month to see how I like traveling by myself, planning my trips, and starting to understand what Clara's life is like.

"Mr. Darwish?" a voice calls from behind me.

I slide my sunglasses down my nose and twist around in the chair. Standing at the water's edge is one of the resort staff, wearing khaki board shorts, flip flops, and a polo with the Wanderlust Resort logo on the breast pocket. He's holding a black tray, the kind he used to bring me a sky juice—my new favorite drink—earlier.

"Sir, you have a call." He holds up the cordless phone from the nearby bar.

My eyebrows draw together in confusion and then worry. Only a few people know how to get a hold of me, and I'm fairly certain they would not be breaking the no-technology rule unless there was good cause.

I haul myself out of the chair and start to drag it up the beach.

"You can leave the chair. I'll take care of it," he tells me with a wave while holding the phone out to me.

"Thanks, Marco." I grab the phone and press it to my ear. I haven't held a phone this big in decades. It's like I've been transported back to the 90s. "Hello?"

"Nash!" It's Uncle D.

"Is everything okay?"

"Completely fine. Peter has been keeping me up to date while you've been gone. He's quiet but a heck of a smart guy. Doesn't let me do anything fun but god damn if he doesn't always have a good reason. I like him."

"What did you want to do this time?"

"I just thought it would be better to default the sort order of the timeline feature."

"And how much time did Peter think that would take for his team to code?"

"Two months!" Uncle D grumbles. That sounds about right. He does, however, launch into a lecture on *why* he thinks it would be better. Marco's still hanging around me, so I gesture for us to move over to the bar where it's shaded, and I can give the phone back to the barkeep when I'm done.

"Well, you got me off track," Uncle D says. "The whole reason I was calling is to ask you to meet with someone for me."

I chew on my lip, wishing I had my phone with me so I could look at my schedule. I hold the receiver away from my mouth and ask the bartender for pen and paper. "When and where? I'll have to see about changing my flight."

"Right now, and in the business center."

Right now? I look down at myself. I'm wearing board shorts. That's it. That's all: no shoes, no shirt, no problem at the resort. "The business center is closed." This was part of the welcome spiel at the front desk for the disconnected weekend.

"Trust me, it's not."

"Who am I meeting with?"

"Oh, good question. Unfortunately, I gotta go. Nash, it's imperative you get to the business center right now. Do not pass go, do not collect two hundred dollars. Going through a tunnel, goodb—"

Uncle D, who is most definitely in his office and *not* going through a tunnel, hangs up on me.

I sigh. I suppose I'm getting dragged back into work. Marco's been hovering nearby, so I ask him where the business center is.

"I can show you the way."

I follow Marco, wondering what crisis I'll find when I get there. I wonder if I should go back to my room first to grab a shirt, but the business center is closer than I expected, and Uncle D said to hurry. I'll duck in, assure whoever it is that I'm here and I'll be back and appropriately dressed in a few minutes. Marco opens the door for me as I come around the corner.

"Thanks, man."

"Enjoy your day, sir."

There's a little hallway, doors on either side, but straight ahead, I can see a slice of a conference room table, and beyond that, a lush jungle view out of big, floor-to-ceiling windows.

I walk into the space and freeze. There, on my right-hand side, is Clara, eyes wide and her body frozen, too.

"Clara?"

"Hey. Um, hi." She smooths her hand down her floral sundress, her gaze flicking down my bare chest and then back up. A smile flits across her face. "I guess I was worried about being underdressed for nothing."

"What are you doing here?" My surprise doesn't overshadow my joy at seeing her—it never does. I expected that the next time I saw her would be months from now, at some family event where we would be awkwardly avoiding each other. This is a good surprise.

She nods at the far side of the room. I follow her gaze and find a glossy folder placed at the head of the table, and I recognize her logo on the cover.

"Have a seat," she says. "Can I get you anything? Water or coffee?" She's deadpanning, but the corners of her lips twitch up in amusement.

"I've just drank a cocktail, so I may not be in the right mindset for a business meeting," I warn her.

She tilts her head, smiling slyly at me. "I don't know, that sounds like a pretty fun business meeting. Don't worry. I won't allow you to make any rash decisions. It's just a pitch."

I take a seat and rest my elbows on the table, steepling my fingers and schooling my face into a look of concentration. "What have you got for me?"

"This is a proposal for a transition period of *Worth Going*." She clicks the remote in her hand and the screen behind her changes. It's a calendar for next month, and there are bars of colors running across various days or weeks, each with the name of a business. I read *Phuket Hot Flights* over one day and *Halong Bay Elemental Resort* blocked out over a whole week. There are blank days, though not many. "Over the next few slides, you'll see the commitments I've made throughout the first few months of this year." She explains a few of the notes, then clicks to March, which is similarly filled out. And then April, which has more blank days than March. The next screen is full of statistics. "I've identified a few opportunities for me to fly back to New York or trips in which it might be appropriate for you to accompany me. Any questions?"

I'm leaning forward now, my arms folded on the tabletop and an amused smile on my face. I've been watching Clara slip from nervous and maybe even embarrassed to confident and thorough. I ask a few questions about locations, as some of these places I've never heard of.

"Next, we'll talk about the financials," she says when I've gotten my geography lesson.

The next few slides cover income, giving me a baseline of information about advertising revenue and commission rates. Clara is impressive—really impressive. Like, she puts some of my teammates to shame, some of my colleagues, and the people outside my company who pitch to me. She's more engaging than ninety-five percent of them.

And more guilt floods in. I wanted Clara to cut back on her business without understanding the full range of what she does. Her job is so hard. I know how much she loves her family, how much she's lost connections with friends. Why did I think that holding on to her was more important than just being with her, no matter how we chose to spend the time?

"Now, this part you may want to pay extra close attention to," Clara says, and I refocus on her, caught.

"I'm a complete dick," I say.

"Well, I wouldn't go that far. I can't blame you for spacing out a little bit at the boring numbers."

Her smile is a little lop-sided, self-deprecating.

"No, I meant that I am a complete dick because of the way I behaved over Christmas. I shouldn't have made the day all about me and what I wanted."

She tilts her head, cocking a hip at me. "I didn't take your suggestions very well either. It's not like you told me how I should change my business or plans. You took me for a day out in the city and told me that you love me and want to spend more time with me." Clara traces her finger over a whirl of wood on the table. "I was thrown off and got scared."

"That's fair," I say. "I took the wrong approach and ignored having the hard conversation for too long. I don't want you to give up anything in your business for me." Clara looks up at me. "What you've built is amazing. You are passionate, and your presentation is perfect. If I was a potential investor, I'd be completely sold."

"Who says you aren't a potential investor?" She smirks and straightens, clicking the remote, guiding my attention back to the screen and returning to business. "Here's my new five-year plan. In the near future, it's built on the foundation of your own suggestion—me living with you when I'm in the city. I'll reduce my number of trips for the rest of the year and spend more time with you."

My heart lurches.

"I'll save on accommodation costs and," Clara continues, "combined with my existing savings, I'll be able to take some time to set up the next iteration of *Worth Going*. Ad revenue and affiliates will shift back, and I'll focus on two projects. The first is organized tours around the world, returning to some of my favorite places or using contacts I've made over the last few years to plan trips to new destinations. The second is a different project. I'm setting up tours in New York, working with immigrants and their communities to spotlight their home countries, all without leaving the city."

Her eyes haven't lost that spark of excitement, but they do soften. "You did show me that I have this great resource directly in front of me. Our day touring the city took me to places I've only dreamed of going, and I think I can make that dream come true for other people, too."

I can't respond with words, so instead, I get up and walk around the table. Clara tilts her head up and my arms slide around her waist as if they've always belonged there. The fabric is thin, the heat of her body radiating through.

"If I'm understanding correctly, you're asking to move in with me?"

Clara places her hands on my biceps. "Is that all you heard?" she scoffs.

"I think it's the most important part." I squeeze her waist, pressing our bodies closer together.

"There is one, teeny tiny other thing," she says.

I lower my head, letting my cheek graze her forehead, and am rewarded with a sharp inhale from her. "What's that?"

"You have to go on some of these trips with me."

"Clara, I'm done trying to make your life fit into mine. That was selfish and short-sighted. This trip is just a start for me. That compromise that I want, I'm ready to hold up my end. I want to take trips with you, and I want to plan some trips with just the two of us to explore places I want to see. I know my job is demanding, but I should take some lessons from Heartly's mission. The things that are good in my life, the things that make me happy, like you, your trips, and your family, they matter the most. And to get to travel with the best tour guide in the world? That's an opportunity I'm unwilling to compromise on."

Clara laughs and swats at my arm, but I capture her up in a kiss. Her giggles die as our bodies turn heated, but I don't let it burn too brightly; I pull back, easing sweet, gentle kisses on her lips. More than anything, I want to disappear with her, run back to my cabana and forget about the blue ocean and white sand and just lose the day with her.

But she probably has taken time out of her busy schedule to come to see me. And it's a little easier to pull back when I know that someday soon, she'll be moving in with me, calling our place home while she's in the city.

I'm elated. And I know this is Clara's idea, but . . .

I pull back and look into her eyes. "Are you sure you're okay with this?"

"Yeah," she says. Her fingers tangle behind my head, and she leans back to see me better. "I've done such amazing travel, but I think in the last few years, it's been getting harder and harder to leave you and my family. I tried to ignore it because I wanted to carry this idea of my mom, the intrepid world traveler, around, but Mom wouldn't have wanted to take one or the other—she wanted both. I'll never give up traveling, and I hope we do lots and lots of trips together. But I'm ready for the next step. And I'm ready to be with you."

We kiss again, her mouth opening under mine and heat flickering through my body until we break apart on a gasp.

"When do you have to leave?" I chase the words back to her lips for more kisses.

"Well, here's another surprise," she says when I finally let her answer. "I reached out to this resort and asked if they wanted to work with me again. They were very willing, especially since I don't need a comped room."

I pull back and inspect the smirk on her face. "What does that mean?"

Her smirk morphs into a grin. "That means you get to see me work."

EPILOGUE - CLARA

THE NEXT DAY, I'VE GOT MY CAMERA OUT AND AM ON THE JOB. "These colors," I breathe. The chef of Wanderlust Resort, Adrian, leans against the railing of the palapa. It's one of his creations that I'm enthralled by, a bright and colorful ceviche set in a martini glass. I am talking about the ceviche, but I'm also talking about the colors behind it—the blue sea extends all the way out to the horizon from here.

"This place certainly is colorful," he says.

"You've worked here a long time, right?" I ask as I click away with my camera. I love talking to staff at these kinds of places, and I remember Adrian from the last time I was here. I almost always glean a little tidbit of information about the location that I might not have gotten from a management team or the marketing brochure.

"Almost eight years," he answers.

There's a slurping of a straw behind me, and I glance back. Nash sits at the bar, and what was a glass of sky juice is now empty.

I roll my eyes at him, chuckling. "You are going to sleep so hard tonight." After my presentation yesterday, we holed up in his cabana—and in his bed. It wasn't that we had non-stop sex—we're not machines, although I did orgasm five times, and yes, he kept count—but we spent the day lazily. It was the kind of day that I'd envisioned for the day after Christmas; we ate energy bars from my backpack for dinner and watched a movie between orgasms.

But, in addition to the sex marathon, Nash is slightly sunburned from hanging out on the beach with me today, and he's had . . . I think he's up to three of these sky juice drinks. I had the bartender show me how to make them so that Nash can enjoy them at home.

Home—his place. The most specific and true home I've had in a long time.

Adrian and I grin conspiratorially at each other, but then his gaze flicks over my shoulder, and that grin morphs into a wide smile.

"Hello," a voice calls out from behind me. I lower my camera and turn around, finding the owner of the resort, a biracial woman about my age, walking up. Emery's in a thin sundress like mine, with corkscrew curls and a smattering of freckles across her face. She offers me her hand. "Great to work with you again, Clara."

"Glad to be back. Thanks for working with me on such late notice."

"You got it." She smiles pleasantly. "Welcome back to Wanderlust Resort." Her gaze shifts to the chef. "Hey, baby."

Adrian meets Emery halfway, and they lean into each other for a kiss on the lips. It's perfunctory, nothing too gauche to be doing in front of clients, but their eyes and smiles are warm.

"How was your trip?" he asks her.

Emery rolls her eyes. "Mom is still pretty pissed at me." She sighs, glancing over at me. "We'll talk later," she tells Adrian. The next words are directed at me. "I just got back from visiting my mom in New York."

"I hope you had fun?"

"I did. It was part business, part pleasure, so that was productive, at least. Speaking of which, did you find your man?" She bats her eyelashes coyly. When she asked why I was coming to the resort, I filled her in on my plan. Emery is smart and savvy, and the last time I was here, we had a great time talking shop over frozen drinks.

"I did," I tilt my head at Nash, still sitting at the bar and watching with amusement. "That's my . . . boyfriend, Nash." *Boyfriend*. That's the first time I've said it out loud to someone.

Emery strides toward the bar, offering Nash her hand. "Nash, welcome, and thanks for. . . ."

The words die on her lips, and in the mirror over the bar, I can see Emery's jaw drop and her outstretched hand sags. For a moment, there's only the sound of the gentle lapping of water at the beach.

"Mr. Darwish!" Emery exclaims. "Oh, what a pleasure to meet you." She raises her hand again, offering a much more enthusiastic handshake now, which Nash accepts. "Oh my god, you're staying here? Has everything been okay? The staff takes good care of you? How's the food been?"

She's still shaking Nash's hand. Adrian comes up behind her, placing his hands on her upper arms and gently detaching her from Nash.

"He's been having a great stay, I promise," Adrian says, pulling her to the side.

"I have. Honestly."

"Are you sure?" Emery calls over her shoulder as Adrian pulls her away, but then he bows his head down, and they have a hushed conversation. Nash and I share an amused glance, and I hear something about the magazine Nash was in.

I walk over to the makeshift studio and get back to work. We're almost done here, and I have plans for an actual dinner out in public with Nash instead of sequestering us in our room again.

And tomorrow, I leave, hopping three flights to get back on schedule for my work.

"Clara, Nash, it was nice to meet you," Emery says, drawing my attention. She's wringing her hands. "Let me know if you need anything. Really. Oh, and we're doing another technology-free weekend for Valentine's Day, in case you want to come back?" Her words tip up, hopeful.

"Tempting, but I already have plans. Maybe next year. Thanks for working with me, Emery, and I hope to see you again before I leave tomorrow."

"You, too." She glances at Nash. "And same to you, Mr. Darwish." She ducks her head and leaves.

"I'm gonna go . . . ," Adrian says, pointing his thumb over his shoulder in the direction Emery went. "I'll be back." He trots off to catch up with Emery.

Nash and I look at each other and burst out laughing. "Okay, okay, this time it was you," I admit.

"The odds have been in my favor," he teases.

I let my camera hang from my neck and step into Nash's space, wrapping my arms around his neck. "The hottest almost-billionaire bachelor? Well, lucky me," I tap the tip of his nose with my finger. "This nutcracker is all mine."

The End

Turn up the heat at the Wanderlust Resort.

Want to read about Emery and Adrian? Their short story, Beach Boss, is free for newsletter subscribers. Download your copy by scanning here:

Newsletter subscribers also get bonus epilogues and a behind-the-scenes look at the trips that inspired my stories.

AUTHOR'S NOTE

My grandmother took me to see *The Nutcracker*, performed by Houston Ballet, for over twenty-five years. I love the idea of doing a retelling and was shocked to find how problematic the original story and performances of *The Nutcracker* were. Houston Ballet had changed many of the issues—for example, Drosselmeyer was a mysterious but kind man, and the Arabic coffee dance was a pas de deux—but it was eye-opening, to say the least.

After all my research for this book, I maintain that Houston Ballet does the best *Nutcracker* in the world, and I will forever miss seeing Lauren Anderson perform as the Sugar Plum Fairy and Randy Herrera as the Russian dancer.

And, of course, seeing the performance with my grandmother.

Reviews are critical to all authors. You can leave a review for
Nutcracker with Benefits at all retailers
Amazon | Apple | Kobo
Barnes & Noble | Google Books
and
Goodreads | BookBub

Also by Liz Alden:

The Love and Wanderlust Series
The Night in Lover's Bay (free prequel short story)
The Fling in Panama
The Slow Burn in Polynesia
The Second Chance in the Mediterranean
The Rival in South Africa (standalone novella)
The Player in New Zealand
The Best Friend in Indonesia (free standalone short story)

Aged Like Fine Wine Series
Rosé with My Fake Fiancé
Riesling with My Roommate
Prosecco with My Professor
Cava with My Colleague

Holiday Retellings Series
Nutcracker with Benefits
Frosty Proximity

Wanderlust Resort Series
Beach Boss (free standalone short story)
Beach Resolution
Put it in Beach Mode

<u>Standalones</u>
The Boudoir Arrangement

ACKNOWLEDGMENTS

I am in awe and thrilled by my readers who have fallen in love with my work. You make a tough and (sometimes) unrewarding job fun. Thank you to Marty Vee and Lillian Lark, who read early versions of this book, and the rest of the many authors in my circle who encouraged and supported me.

And as always, a big thank-you to my husband, who encouraged me so much from day one, and my parents, all five of them, who supported this book in one way or another.

To Lober: Thank you for supporting the arts and encouraging me to support them, too. The Nutcracker isn't the same without you.

ABOUT LIZ ALDEN

Liz Alden is a digital nomad. Most of the time she's on her sailboat, but sometimes she's in Texas. She knows exactly how big the world is—having sailed around it—and exactly how small it is, having bumped into friends worldwide.

She's been a dishwasher, an engineer, a CEO, and occasionally gets paid to write or sail.

The books are inspired by her real-life travel.

Follow Liz:

9 781954 705203